CRYPTID KILLERS 2

HYBRID HELL

ALISTER HODGE

SEVERED PRESS
HOBART TASMANIA

CRYPTID KILLERS

WWW.SEVEREDPRESS.COM

ISBN: 978-1-922861-66-5

CHAPTER ONE

Kevin swung open the passenger door and stepped straight into a putrefying mound of roadkill, his foot plunging deep into a dead wallaby's abdomen. Swollen with gas, the gut deflated with the sound of a wet fart.

You gotta be kidding me...

The stench hit the back of his throat like a physical entity, rank and thick. Saliva flooded Kevin's mouth. He lunged sideways, spewing over the corpse and down the inside of the door.

"What the fuck, man?" said Paul. "This is my mum's car!"

Kevin hung out the doorway with spit drooling from his lips, waiting for his stomach to heave again. *'My mum's car.' Fucking loser.*

He was hardly a catch himself. Thirty-six, unemployed and living with his dad; Kevin didn't even have a driving licence, let alone a car of his own. Finally, he wiped his mouth and spat into the dark.

"It's your fault, dickhead. You parked over roadkill."

Kevin pulled his foot from the corpse and stepped over the mound of decaying flesh. Turning on the flashlight of his mobile phone, a second wave of nausea hit as he saw the mess on his trainers. Green and brown scunge covered his left shoe and ankle, cold goop oozing amongst the laces and down the top of his sock. He wiped off the worst of it against a tussock of grass, breathing through his mouth in an attempt to avoid the smell.

While Kevin fussed over his shoe, Paul moved the car and cleaned the vinyl interior with a handful of tissues. Giving up on his runners, Kevin pulled two rucksacks from the boot and began a last-minute check of their equipment.

The two men had met through an online group of true believers, people with a common faith that the Tasmanian tiger still existed. An apex predator, the carnivorous marsupial had the build of a short-haired wolf, with black stripes across its back and rump interspersed by sandy-coloured fur. Scientifically known as the thylacine, the last verified specimen had died at Hobart Zoo in 1936, with the species declared officially extinct in 1986. Despite this, unverified sightings continued to fuel rumours of its survival in the Tasmanian wilderness.

Seeing everything in place, he gave a satisfied nod and shouldered his pack. Kevin extracted a GoPro camera from his jacket pocket and passed it to Paul. He hadn't been able to afford a recent model suited to night filming, but it would have to do.

"Let's do the intro here," said Kevin. He paused to straighten his beanie and smooth a patchy growth of hair above his upper lip.

"You got to shave the bum fluff, mate," said Paul, lifting the camera. "Fourteen-year-olds can grow better moustaches."

Kevin just scowled. "Cut the crap and hit record, will you?" He shrugged off his annoyance and stared into the camera.

"Thanks for joining us, fellow tiger hunters! Hold on to your hats, because tonight we're about to see a *live* thylacine." Kevin glanced over his shoulder into the darkness. "About two hundred metres into the bush behind me is a private research facility. Owned by a company called Naturtech, they're known to investigate the disfiguring malady affecting our beloved Tasmanian devils in a hope it might be cured. However, I believe there's a second undeclared research program in action.

"Over the last two years, Naturtech have significantly increased the facility's security. With fences topped by razor wire, CCTV and automated gates, it could pass for a military installation." Kevin's tone dropped to a conspiratorial whisper as he leaned close to the camera. "I discovered they have a national grant to resurrect the Tasmanian tiger, using DNA from a preserved specimen at the National Museum of Australia. And why else would they need such security unless they'd had success?" He stepped back again.

"Last week I flew a drone over the facility, and what do you think I saw? A vast complex of laboratories, breeding sheds and exercise pens. Short story; everything needed to grow a thylacine joey to adulthood, ready for reintroduction to the wild.

"And today," said Kevin, pausing for dramatic effect. "Today we will share the *first* film of a Tasmanian tiger since 1936!" he glanced at Paul behind the camera, cheeks flushed with excitement. "Let's do this!"

***

"Well I'll be fucked," said Paul, staring up at the cyclone wire blocking their path. "There *actually is* razor-wire topping that fence."

"I told you this place was dodgy," said Kevin.

"Are you certain about the thylacines?" Paul dumped his pack on the ground. "Facilities like this don't take kindly to trespassers. If we get caught, they'll drag us to court and sue."

"Of course, I'm bloody sure. If you're too much of a pussy to help, wait for me here," muttered Kevin. "But I guarantee, you'll be kicking yourself later."

He extracted a set of bolt cutters from his pack and began snipping through the steel lattice, creating a hole at the bottom of the fence. Hands shaking from the effort, Kevin pulled up one side, creating a horizontal mouth at ground level.

"You coming or not?"

Paul stared at the opening before suddenly jerking into action. He dropped to his belly and crawled through the gap. "We better not get caught, my mum will freaking kill me if I end up in jail."

Kevin waited for Paul to hold the fence, then crawled to the other side. For all his bravado, Kevin's heart was beating like a maniac. He'd never even jaywalked, let alone committed break-and-enter. A smile split his face as he rode the adrenaline surge. Even if they didn't find a tiger, it was going to make one hell of a story.

The pair stumbled through undergrowth, twigs and spiked grasses dragging at their clothes until they reached a small clearing. Eucalypt branches arced overhead, obscuring the heavens and cloaking the area in shadow. Kevin squatted and shined his torch at a small pile of scat. Elongated in shape, it definitely didn't belong to a wallaby or Tasmanian devil. This meant they had to be in one of the enclosures. Hand shaking with excitement, he scooped the pile of faeces into a clip-lock bag for later examination.

Kevin stood again, his thighs aching from the unaccustomed exercise, and shone a torch about the clearing. "This'll do us nicely, yeah?" For ten paces in either direction, there was nothing but leaves and grass. If they enticed a thylacine into frame, it would provide an unobstructed photo opportunity.

Kevin soon had the tripod, camera and motion-activated light source assembled. Satisfied, he brushed dirt from his knees and walked over to inspect Paul's work. Three dismembered rabbits littered the ground, bits of leaves sticking to the bloodied joints. Paul upended a plastic carrier bag of blood and entrails, adding a heady tang of copper and shit to the bait.

Paul wiped his hands on a scrap of old tea-towel and flicked the switch on a small Bluetooth speaker. A high-pitched scream of injured rabbits burst from the unit, causing a bird to lift from its roost on frightened wings.

The two men retreated to the edge of the clearing, eyes fixed on the butchered meat in hope.

***

Kevin squatted on the ground, arse crack showing above his jeans. He glanced at his watch and grimaced. Thirty minutes waiting with nothing to show for it. Suddenly the sensor-light flashed, drenching the foreground in brilliant white. As the glow faded, Kevin saw a streak of brown leaving the clearing. Excitedly he stood and made for the camera, pins and needles tingling his legs from the abrupt change in position. Paul launched into motion at the same time, darting forward to switch off the speaker and rearrange the baits. Without the painful recording, the surrounding bush became deathly quiet.

Kevin scrolled through a burst of photos taken by the GoPro. A crease furrowed his brows. *That can't be right... It's too big.* He went through them again, confusion battling excitement at what they'd caught on film. The creature was twice the size of what he'd expected, standing over waist height at the shoulder.

"Hey Paul, you need to take a look at this—"

A guttural bark sounded from the trees to the right. Gooseflesh puckered Kevin's arms as his head flicked to the sound, eyes searching the darkness. A shadow broke cover, stalking toward Paul. Growls, interspersed by high whines began to emanate from the circumference of the clearing.

Shit, there's more than one.

Kevin looked down at the image on the screen again, drawn to the thylacine's distinctive markings. A growl vibrated from the dark to his left, closer this time. Kevin glanced sideways. Thylacines closed from multiple directions like wraiths in the dark, striped backs melding with the shadows. His gut twisted as he realised the beasts weren't coming for the rabbits.

Oblivious, Paul reset the bait while grinning like a fool. "Did we catch a photo?"

Instead of warning his friend of the impending attack, Kevin lifted the GoPro and hit record. Paul cried out in surprised confusion as a huge thylacine smashed into his back, knocking him onto his face. It leapt onto Paul's shoulders and ripped a bloodied patch of material from his jacket. Paul screamed, a terrified cry of agony.

Another thylacine slashed in from the side and bit Paul's exposed hand, worrying at the fingers. The first snarled and snapped at it, refusing to give up its prize.

"Help!" Paul stared up at his mate, eyes wide and pleading, pupils dilated. "Please!"

Kevin stumbled back a step, telling himself there was nothing he could do. A third creature joined the feast. Bigger than the first two, it clamped wide jaws about Paul's neck. It violently shook its head, tearing deep lacerations with its canines. Arterial blood spurted from his decimated carotids, splashing over the chest and jowls of the beast.

Paul thrashed on the ground, breath gurgling through a torn throat. Finally the man fell still, his cries replaced by the repulsive sound of feeding. Powerful jaws crunched through bone and cartilage alike, mouthfuls of fat and muscle gagged down without chewing.

Kevin glanced behind, searching in the dark for the fence line. Breath tight in his chest, he began to ease away. Ten paces back he turned, ready to run—and stepped on a dry branch. Kevin froze, pulse loud as a drum in his ears. He looked over his shoulder at the feasting predators, praying they had somehow missed the noise. The largest creature swallowed another mouthful, turned his way and sniffed the air. Lips snarled back as it detected his scent.

A strangled moan of fear erupted from Kevin's lips, hot urine flooding his thighs. He dropped the GoPro in the dirt and ran, sprinting for the fence and safety. The beasts gave chase, excitedly barking as they tore through the undergrowth in pursuit. Kevin pushed his legs as fast as they would go, arms pumping and air harsh in his throat. His foot caught on a fallen branch and he fell, tumbling head over heels. A rock gouged Kevin's forehead, tearing a flap tissue so that the periosteum shone white. Heedless to the blood sheeting his face, he lurched to his feet and ran on.

Kevin slapped into the cyclone wire of the fence. He looked down, searching in vain for the hole they had created. Kevin glanced over his shoulder, saw yipping shadows streak under the trees towards him. There was no time to search for the hole, he'd have to risk the razor wire at the top. Kevin leapt, wrapping fingers into the wire links to drag himself higher. A thylacine smashed into his leg, taking his calf in a vice-like grip. Fearsome canines punctured his jeans, plunging deep into the muscle.

Kevin screamed. Looking down, he saw the creature hanging off his leg. It began to thrash, shaking its head viciously from side to side to rip him off the fence. Kevin held on for his life as the wire sliced deep, cutting down to the tendons. Another beast jumped and bit his ankle. The combined weight of the two huge animals was too much and suddenly Kevin was falling.

Stars burst as his head thudded onto the ground, pain exploding like a hot poker from a cracked skull. The fall had dislodged the thylacines from his legs and they began to circle their cornered prey. More of the beasts trotted in from the bush until he was surrounded by a group of twelve. Somewhere in the back of his mind, Kevin queried their numbers. Thylacines didn't hunt in packs. This shouldn't be happening; the *whole attack* shouldn't be happening. Blood pooled from Kevin's ruined legs as he dragged himself back, retreating until the fence pressed against his spine. Three of the beasts padded slowly forward, lips retracted in a growl.

Kevin leaned forward and screamed at them, waving his arms to scare them away. The largest of the three paused for a moment, then lunged and bit into his thigh. The other two joined him, one going for his soft abdomen, the other his arm. Kevin's eyes bulged with agony, his scream echoing beneath the trees as the pack began to feed.

CHAPTER TWO

"Dad, can I have some pocket money?" asked Beth. "Mum said you can afford more than you're giving us."

Eoin Carter raised an eyebrow at his oldest daughter as he passed her bag from the car boot. At ten years of age, Beth had started pushing the boundaries. "I highly doubt that, love. Your mum and I still communicate pretty well. She would have said if there was an issue."

"Fine," muttered Beth. She took her backpack and left in a sulk.

Carter frowned with annoyance but let her walk away, not wanting to end their week in a fight. Instead, he turned and hung his old army duffle bag over the shoulder of his youngest daughter, Chloe. Carter watched his girls walk up the driveway to their mother's house. The older child ran inside without a backward glance, but the younger took her time. At six years old, the duffle bag dwarfed her small frame. Chloe stopped halfway and turned around.

"Are you coming, Daddy?"

"Sorry kiddo, there's a few things I have to do."

Chloe frowned but nodded acceptance as she climbed the porch steps. The front door opened and his ex-wife, Kim, stepped out. Carter forced an amicable smile and raised a hand to wave, but needn't have bothered. Kim didn't even look his way before shooing Chloe inside and closing the door.

Carter sighed and climbed behind the wheel. Truth be told, he had no immediate plans. But since Kim's new partner had moved in, he preferred to give them space. Seeing his ex-wife in the arms of a new man sucked. He could maintain the required niceties and be civil, but it always sunk him into a dark mood with a need for a drink.

Amongst his army mates, dislocated families and alcoholism had become the depressing standard. Several tours with the Australian SAS in Afghanistan and Iraq had broken his marriage. The situation had been tough on Kim; tasked with child rearing alone, she'd felt abandoned. Eventually she'd had enough and posted divorce papers while he was in Afghanistan.

Carter turned the key in the ignition and pulled away from the curb. He'd taken two weeks annual leave over the school holiday break. Spending the first week with his daughters, Carter had planned on taking the second week for himself. He'd thought to read some books, hit the gym and finally dip his toe in the dating game. But after seeing his kids walk away, Carter knew he'd be soon pacing his flat, stuck inside his head with negative thoughts spiralling.

Carter hooked a phone from his pocket and dialled Agent Rylan. Medically discharged from the SAS with a hip full of shrapnel, he'd transferred to the Australian Security Intelligence Organisation (ASIO) and been assigned to the Cryptid Investigation Unit. Run by veteran agent Sophia Rylan, his first months in the unit introduced a world of freakish creatures he'd never known existed. And at times wished he still didn't.

Rylan picked up on the first ring. "What the fuck, Carter? You're on leave. Piss off and enjoy it." A dial tone sounded as she hung up.

Carter shook his head, pulled his car to the roadside and punched in her number again. Rylan had zero patience for polite conversation, but then again, if he'd been alive for hundreds of years like her, he'd have given society the middle finger long ago. *A cryptid running the Cryptid Investigation Unit.* The thought still made him shake his head.

This time, he talked immediately. "You got any cases in progress?"

Rylan sighed. "It's Sunday morning, which means you've probably just dropped the girls back at Kim's, right? Look, there's healthier ways to distract yourself than working, Carter. Go see a movie, download Tinder or something. There's got to be some airheads who get weak at the knees for old battle scars, right?"

"Don't be a dick," muttered Carter. "Is there a job going or not?"

"Fine." Rylan barked a short laugh at his injured tone. "I'm in Hobart. If you're desperate, there's some species surveillance you could help with. Get yourself an afternoon flight and we'll talk tonight."

***

Carter dumped his bag on the hotel bed and walked to a window overlooking Salamanca Square. He'd little trouble acquiring a flight, landing in Hobart by mid-afternoon. He brushed his right hand along sandstone bordering the window, rough-hewn blocks coarse under his fingers. For an Australian building, it was old. Built in 1840 as a ship's chandlery, it had sold nautical equipment to whalers and other commercial vessels at the nearby wharf. Hosting various businesses over the years, the most recent face-lift had transformed the premises to a hotel.

Daylight faded outside, long shadows stretching across the pavement. Multiple bars and restaurants lined the square, slowly filling with patrons. Those seated outside in the brisk evening gravitated to the pedestal heaters dotted between tables. If Rylan didn't have much work going, he'd be happy to sink a few local brews while people watching. Anything was better than sitting alone in an empty house.

Carter glanced at his watch and realised he needed to get moving. He completed a safety check on his Glock and stored it in a shoulder holster, shrugged a jacket on over the top and left his room. Opting for the stairs, Carter soon emerged into a bar and restaurant on the ground floor. Leather armchairs the colour of aged tobacco clustered around small tables. He paused for a moment, scanning the room until he spotted Rylan seated near a window. She sat with a half-empty glass in hand, staring into space above an open book. He grabbed two pints of cascade lager from the bar and wandered over.

Carter placed one of the pints before her and took a seat. "How goes it?"

Rylan nodded thanks, downed the last of her pint and picked up the new one. "Yeah, I'm alright, but reading this stuff is a little depressing." She closed the book in hand and placed it on the table.

A wolf-like creature with a striped back graced the cover, an unmistakeable rendering of the Tasmanian tiger. Titled "A Short History of the Thylacine", Carter opened the book to a random page, landing on a black and white photo of a thylacine. The last of its kind in captivity, the animal had died at Hobart's Beaumaris Zoo in 1936. Left in a bare concrete enclosure, it had perished from exposure to extreme winter weather conditions.

"So many Australian species have become extinct," said Carter, staring at the photo. The unfortunate creature looked cold, lonely and bored.

"Yep," Rylan nodded. "And it's worse to know you played a role in their demise."

Carter gave her a questioning look but remained quiet. He'd quickly learnt that if Rylan wanted to talk about something from her lengthy past, she would speak in her own time.

Born in England sometime in the early 1700s, Rylan had grown to adulthood before her unique genetic traits became apparent. As those about her turned grey and stooped with age, she'd retained the body of a woman in her prime. Mixed admiration and jealousy from her neighbours had eventually morphed to fear and whispers of the occult as the years progressed. For how else could a person ignore the ravages of time, if not by a deal with the devil?

Fleeing accusations of witchcraft, Rylan found there were few options for single women to earn a living outside a brothel. And so, she'd chosen a different horror. With head shaved and her breasts bound, Rylan disguised herself as a man to enter the military.

Amongst the slaughter of old battlefields, it had been relatively easy to move between units, and from one theatre of war to another without people noting her longevity. She'd been shot and injured many times, and yet her wounds knitted at lightning speed, denying eternal rest from traumas that should have proved mortal. Her current role with ASIO was her first step outside the military in some time. It had taken Carter a while to get his head around Rylan's past, and if he hadn't seen her re-animate and re-grow a severed hand on their first mission together, he wouldn't believe a word of it.

"After the Boer War ended I needed time away from the military," said Rylan, staring into her beer. "Britain employed brutal tactics to crush the enemy. We burnt farms and crops, corralling thousands of Boer women and children in concentration camps to die of starvation and disease. When the war finally ended, I wanted to forget the part I'd played. I took an honourable discharge and travelled as far away from England as I could, ending up in Tasmania of all places."

Carter glanced at the book in his hand, starting to put the dots together. "So, you were here when thylacines were still alive. Did you ever see one?"

"Yeah. Saw them, killed them as well." Rylan took a deep swallow from her pint. "At the time, we thought they were some kind of Australian wolf. Sheep farmers blamed them for killing lambs and the state introduced a one-pound bounty for every thylacine culled."

Carter flicked through a couple of pages, coming to a yellowed photo of a hunter posing by two thylacine carcases. "Was that a lot of money back then?"

Rylan nodded. "Nearly a week's wage for your average worker and hard for someone like me to ignore. I had a rifle, could track and shoot with the best of them. And after contributing to the destruction of so many families in the Transvaal, I thought it was penance to help a different group of poor farmers. Turns out, I just helped wipe out an innocent species."

"You couldn't have known at the time."

Rylan shrugged. "Doesn't make it feel any better. Nature once seemed endless, *indestructible*. And now, every second species is facing extinction while the forests dwindle, and the seas become glutted with plastic. It hit me pretty hard when the last thylacine died a few decades later."

Carter thumbed over a few more pages, arriving at a scheme to resurrect the species. "Well, this might cheer you up. A research group's confident they can bring thylacines back from the grave." He glanced up, a smile hooking one corner of his mouth. "A 'Jurassic Park' down under, if you will?"

"Fingers crossed, eh?" Rylan took another sip of her drink. "On a different topic, I'll be attending a meeting tomorrow near Port Arthur."

Carter closed the book and sat back in his chair. "The old convict gaol?"

Rylan nodded. "It attracts a few cryptid species I like to keep an eye on. While I'm stuck in the meeting, I want you to do a recce of the site."

"What will I be searching for?"

"The beast's about a metre or so long, has a reptilian body and is attracted to misery." For the first time that afternoon, a grin lit Rylan's face. "Oh, and they're near invisible to the naked eye."

"Sounds like a walk in the park," said Carter, his voice thick with sarcasm.

CHAPTER THREE

Anton stared at the computer screen, concentration slipping for the hundredth time. He pushed his chair back from the desk and spun to face the window behind. Located on the third floor of the main research block, his office window provided an expansive view of eucalypt forest, stretching in unbroken bushland to the coast.

Ignoring the million-dollar view, Anton instead stared at his reflection. It had been four years since he took over the reins as CEO of Naturtech. Four years of worry, gambles and setbacks until he'd finally achieved success. Anton's lip curled in distaste at his appearance. Grey hairs speckled his scalp, while his once smooth forehead had developed deep frown lines. He smoothed fingers over the bags beneath his eyes, trying to push out the oedema. If he pulled off the deal with Scarpoint, all the long nights would be worth it. He'd be set for life, able to afford cosmetic surgery to repair his ruined appearance and retire to a Caribbean paradise.

A hurried knock sounded at his office door. Anton sighed and turned his chair around. The head animal-keeper stood in his doorway. Face pale beneath a deep tan, he gripped the door handle like a lifeline.

"Whatever you want, Nick, it can wait. We have two benefactors arriving today, and I need to finish preparations."

Nick shook his head. "The girls have got into trouble overnight, Anton. You're going to need to see this."

Anton swore under his breath, but pushed back his chair and tailed the keeper outside. A man of few words, such a request from Nick was unusual. He came with extensive zoological experience, having managed various dangerous animals from grizzly bears to saltwater crocodiles. And he'd never seen him rattled like this.

***

"Jesus," muttered Anton. "Is that what I think it is?" Suddenly feeling very hot, he extracted a hanky from his breast pocket and dabbed a speckling of sweat from his forehead.

"I wish it wasn't," said Nick. The half-eaten remains of two adults lay beside a pair of backpacks and camera equipment. "I gathered everything I could find. It has to be the work of our thylacines. The lock to their building was open this morning, so they had the range of the enclosure overnight."

"Maybe it was wild dogs?" Anton knew he was grasping at straws.

"What, with three metre fences enclosing the reserve? Not a chance, boss. This was the work of our pack, right down to the way they cracked the femurs to access the marrow."

Nick pointed out a bloody trail of disturbed undergrowth and leaves heading toward the perimeter. "I found one of them by the fence ripped to pieces, limbs torn at the joints like they'd played tug-of-war with the body. Had to drag him here in multiple parts."

Anton grimaced. The two heads were largely untouched except for a few lacerations, more than enough for photo identification. Not that he had any plans of that. The bastards should have kept their noses out of other people's business.

"Should we call the cops?"

Anton stared at the animal keeper, face aghast. "Are you a fucking idiot? No one knows our thylacines even exist."

"But the government supplied part of the funding, gave ethics approval. We'd be in the clear if we declare it. No different to that stupid bastard who climbed into the lion's enclosure at Melbourne Zoo a few years back."

"Do you want to see our animals euthanised? Because that's what would happen." Anton was almost shouting now. "They'll be declared unfit for reintroduction to the wild, a danger to society and slaughter them like stray dogs."

Anton forced himself to stop, take a breath and calm down. It was yet another problem to be solved, just like the multitude of others he'd overcome to get this far.

"You said their access to the larger enclosure was open last night?"

Nick broke eye contact, looking at the ground.

"We both know it's your responsibility to check the enclosures in the evening. What happened, did you get on the drink a little earlier than usual last night?"

Nick swallowed nervously but said nothing.

"Yeah, thought as much. If this got out, I bet you'd face manslaughter charges for such negligence. Do not talk about this to *anyone*, our staff or otherwise."

"Okay, so what do we do with the bodies?"

"Dump the bodies in the Tasmanian devil enclosure. They'll do a better job than pigs in consuming the lot. Burn the clothes."

"And the camera?"

Anton picked up the GoPro with a hanky covering his fingers, careful to avoid touching any blood. "I'll dispose of it."

Yes, he would eventually crush and destroy it, but not before he downloaded its contents. If it showed his thylacines mid hunt, Scarpoint would pay to see them in action.

"And there… there's something else you should know."

Nick took an involuntary step back as Anton fixed him with a glare. "What?"

"One of the adults, Number six, is missing,"

Fuck. "Isn't that the runt of the litter?"

"She's still the size of a great dane. Look, I was hoping she's roaming the enclosure, but there's a chance she might have escaped."

Anton froze, waiting for Nick to continue.

"About twenty metres from the corpse, I found a hole in the fence with the wire levered up. Must have been where these dumb bastards got in. I've already fixed it, but there was a clump of fur attached to one of the wire ends. She might have crawled through the gap."

Anton swore viciously and kicked at one of the heads, a cheekbone caving under the toe of his boot.

Bodies he could hide, but a thylacine on the loose could prove difficult.

CHAPTER FOUR

Rylan parked beside Naturtech's gate, tyres crunching in the gravel as she came to a stop. A plume of dust kicked up by her passage caught up with her, enveloping the car in a cloud of yellow before the wind swept it away. Towering eucalypt forest crowded either side of the narrow access lane. Branches met overhead, reducing the sky to a speckling of blue between leaves. The facility kept a low profile, eschewing physical signage or an online presence.

Rylan sat behind the wheel, allowing herself a moment of satisfaction. A few hundred years of life had taught her many things, one of them being how to play the stock market. With accounts in various countries, she had accumulated huge sums of money, enabling her to anonymously fund research and charities where she could make a difference. Naturtech was one such facility that existed through her financial backing.

Surrounded by national park on all sides, she'd secured the land forty years prior to rehabilitate injured native animals. When a facial tumour disease emerged in the Tasmanian devil population, Rylan used the site to research a solution. Immunotherapy eventually identified a cure to the disease, prompting Naturtech to change direction again, this time seeking to resurrect the Tasmanian tiger. It had been over three years since her last visit. Preferring a hands off approach, when a project appeared on track, she gave her team the freedom to work independently, relying upon progress reports to free her time.

Rylan climbed out of the car and straightened her clothes, steam pluming from her mouth. Despite being early afternoon and remarkably dry for a winter's day, it was freezing. Heavy clouds blocked the sun's warmth and made it seem much later in the day. She stared up for a moment, an eyebrow raised in query. A three metre high cyclone wire barrier stretched from either side of the gate into the bush. A border fence she could understand, but razor wire topping was overkill.

Rylan walked to a small intercom box and depressed a button for security. A guard promptly answered her call and after examining her ID via camera, asked her to wait at the front gate.

What a waste of money and resources.

Rylan turned away from the camera, irritated by the unnecessary obstacle. She'd seen less security on some military bases. Rylan flipped up the lapels of her woollen trench coat and shoved her hands deep into the pockets. She'd come dressed for the part today. Fully expecting a tour of the facility and enclosures, Rylan had ditched the business skirt in lieu of comfort and practicality, wearing a smart suit and pants with flat soled shoes.

The low rumble of an engine grew in volume, and she turned to see an open-roofed Jeep approaching from the other side of the gate. As it neared, the gate kicked into gear and began to slide open along its track. The Jeep pulled to a stop a few meters away and a security guard stepped leisurely from the vehicle. He raised his sunglasses, eyes travelling up her body, pausing at her chest before finally reaching her face with a leer of approval.

"Ms Sophia Rylan, I take it?"

Rylan gave a curt nod and walked to the passenger seat.

"A pleasant surprise *indeed.*" The security guard lowered his sunglasses again and regained his seat behind the wheel. "To be honest, I was expecting someone a little older, ma'am."

Rylan sighed. "And I expected professional behaviour from an employee, not to be ogled on arrival. Consider this your first warning."

The guard's leer disappeared in an instant, his body stiffening to formality. "My apologies, ma'am." He promptly turned the Jeep around and accelerated down the road.

"Better," muttered Rylan. "When was the perimeter upgraded? The automatic gates, cameras and razor wire are new."

"Eighteen months ago."

"Who approved it?"

The guard shrugged. "Someone higher up the chain than me. I just monitor the cameras and keep out unwelcome guests."

Rylan's lips thinned. Her list of questions for Naturtech's general manager, Anton, was growing by the minute. A guttural scream rose above the diesel engine of the Jeep, drawing her attention to an enclosure of Tasmanian devils. There were few sounds like it. Early colonisers of the island had named the animal after hearing its nightmarish calls in the dead of night. Devils usually scavenged under the cover of darkness, fighting over roadkill and rotting carrion, so it was odd for them to be active during the day.

They parked before the first of Naturtech's buildings a few minutes later. Rylan gave a brief nod of thanks to the guard and ascended a short flight of steps to the entrance. A receptionist opened the door, beckoning her inside with a smile.

"Ms Rylan, welcome back to Naturtech. Anton is slightly delayed but will be down in a few minutes." She waved her toward an assortment of delicate pastries, plunger coffee and tea. "In the meantime, please make yourself at home."

Rylan poured a cup of black coffee, blew steam off the surface and took a sip. Pleasantly surprised at the quality, she turned to take in the room. As an entrance hall to the facility, it was large enough to house a small conference or host charity dinners to wine and dine potential donars. Floor to ceiling windows panelled one side of the room, allowing in light and providing a view of the bush. A middle-aged man was the only other person in the room. After casting a brief glance her way, he returned his attention to the view.

Rylan began a slow circuit of the room, studying various photos and paintings of Tasmanian wildlife. Unsurprisingly, thylacines took precedence, with numerous black and white photos from the late 1800s and early 1900s. She paused at one, her gut twisting at recognition of the scene. Ten thylacines hung from a country fence, eyes dry and sightless under the sun's glare. Hind paws tied to the top line of wire, they ranged in size from infant to adult breeding stock, multiple generations killed in a single day. The hunter responsible stood beside them, rifle in hand, face blurred and out of focus. Although the person was unnamed, Rylan knew the hunter in the photo was herself. Using a Lee-Enfield rifle souvenired from the Boer War, she'd just returned from a successful hunt when a reporter from the Hobart Gazette asked to take her photo. She'd earnt ten quid in bounties that day, nearly a month's wage at the time. Rylan turned away from the photo and found a table to ditch her coffee, her stomach turned sour.

"Sophia and Marat!" said Anton, sweeping into the room. His face was flushed, smile wide and fake. "Thank you for joining me today, it is a pleasure to see you both."

The man in the suit wandered over from the window to shake Anton's hand.

"Ms Rylan, have you and Marat been introduced?"

Rylan gave a slight shake of her head in the negative.

"Then let me set that straight." Anton glanced towards the businessman. "This is Marat Drakar from Scarpoint Industries. Scarpoint have generously contributed funds to our research programs over the past two years.

"And Marat, can I introduce you to Ms Rylan, our founding donar and patron. I swear she hasn't aged a day in all the time I've known her—I only wish I knew her skin-care regime!"

"Mr Drakar." Rylan ignored the compliment and briefly clasped Marat's hand. "I confess I'm surprised at your interest. I thought Scarpoint was a private military company?"

Marat smiled, the expression failing to reach his eyes. "You are correct, ma'am, we are proud to be Europe's largest private provider of military personnel. At this moment, our soldiers can be found in operations across Africa, the Middle East and South America."

"Don't forget Europe," said Rylan suppressing a grimace of distaste. "I hear Russia's few successes in the Ukraine are thanks to Scarpoint troops." Rylan hated working with private military contractors. When you fought for the highest bidder, ethics became superfluous. "Why the interest in our extinct thylacine?"

"Unfortunately, it is a matter of public image," laughed Marat. "Although governments are happy to use our soldiers, few are keen to publicly acknowledge our association. So, by supporting various environmental initiatives, we seek to demonstrate our company has a conscience, that we are actually in the business of making the world a better place."

Rylan could buy the public image campaign, but that they were a company who sought to improve the world? Hardly. She pondered his accent, struggling to pin it down. She'd met numerous soldiers like him. Men and women who'd spent decades fighting their way around the world until their original accent became distorted. She was one of them herself.

"Let's start, shall we?" Anton waved them into a meeting room with a smartboard. "We have some exciting developments to share."

He waited for Marat and Rylan to take a seat before tapping the board to change the slide. A graphic of DNA spiralled across the screen. "Our early work mapped the thylacine genome using tissue samples obtained from a preserved specimen. Initial attempts to use this DNA were thwarted by degraded gene segments, however, thanks to advances pioneered by Naturtech, we have successfully repaired these sections and implanted an egg into a relative of the thylacine – the Tasmanian devil."

"So, the gene splices we provided worked?"

Anton nodded. "They certainly did." He tapped the smartscreen again, bringing up a video showing a needle entering a cell under huge magnification. "Using a similar technique to cloning, we transferred thylacine DNA from a somatic cell into a devil's egg cell that has had its nucleus and DNA removed. The egg was then implanted into a tassie devil's uterus to grow."

Rylan sat forward in her chair. "Just a second, are you saying Naturtech's already progressed to the stage of growing a foetus?"

"Multiple, actually," said Anton with a grin. "And once our infant thylacines, also known as 'joeys', reach maturity, the need for surrogates will become obsolete."

Marat clapped his hands enthusiastically. "Excellent work. Unfortunately, I'm on a tight schedule today; may we see the animals?"

Anton turned the smartboard off. "It would be my pleasure." He paused theatrically for a moment. "Aside from our team, you will be the first to see a live thylacine in nearly a century. Are you excited?"

Rylan couldn't help but smile, a buzz of anticipation in her chest. The last time she'd seen a

Tasmanian tiger, it had been over the sights of a rifle.

Anton opened the door with a flourish. “Follow me!”

CHAPTER FIVE

Jan looked up from washing the breakfast dishes as the screen door banged shut. Her partner, Greg, stood there crestfallen. He leaned against the wall with bloodied hands at his sides, small white feathers stuck to pants and shirt.

Jan grabbed a tea towel to dry her hands and stepped around the kitchen bench. "It's happened again, hasn't it?"

He gave a sad nod.

Damn! This was the third time a fox had attacked Greg's prize hens, birds he'd bred over the course of two decades and loved as much as her. He was good at it too. Competing against other chicken fanciers at the Royal Hobart Show, Greg usually came home with a winning ribbon.

"How many?"

"All of them."

Her jaw dropped. "But foxes don't hunt during the day, they were all there this morning."

He shrugged. "It must have attacked while we were out." Tears welled in Greg's eyes for the first time in their long marriage, a sight more disturbing to Jan than the blood on his hands.

Jan pushed open the screen door and strode into the back garden, wanting to see for herself. They lived on a small parcel of land backing onto the bush, an acre block encompassing a huge veggie patch and room for Greg's chooks to scratch about during the day. The back of their property was framed by a green murraya hedge that climbed two or three metres into the air and helped dissuade the chickens from exploring too far. Greg had given up trying to maintain it years before, and now it was almost as wide as it was high. Jan pulled on her gumboots and walked down a dirt path towards the chicken coop, Greg trailing behind.

A break in the weather gifted a blue sky dotted by wisps of cloud. Having left her jumper inside, Jan was glad of the sun's feeble warmth on her arms. She rounded a garden bed of broccoli and stopped dead.

"Jesus…"

Foxes often killed more than they could eat, but this was ridiculous. Fifteen mangled chickens lay sprawled across the grass. Some were barely touched, others in pieces.

"I found four or five out here," said Greg. "But most were in the coop."

Jan toed a dead chicken with her boot, grimacing at the squelch of blood under her feet. The body was torn in half. "Are you sure it was a fox?"

"Has to be. Haven't been any wild dogs for years!" Pink flushed his cheeks as he stared at his dead birds.

Something caught Jan's eye. She pointed out a handful of feathers and flattened grass at the base of the murraya. "Looks like it crawled through the hedge."

Greg rushed over and peered into the shadows beneath. "I think the bastard's still in there! Jan, grab me the spade, will ya."

Jan took the spade leaning against the chicken coop and carried it to her husband. “What are you doing?”

“I’m going to brain the bloody thing!”

Ignoring the wet grass, Greg lay on his belly and wormed his way under the greenery until only his legs showed. A growl sounded from deeper in the hedge, a deep sound more akin to dog than a fox.

“Kill my fuckin’ chickens, will ya,” muttered Greg as he shoved the spade forward. Something yelped. Branches creaked and snapped as the animal changed position within the hedge. A deep throated growl came again, coarse and loud.

“Ah, shit…” Suddenly Greg started scrabbling backwards, abandoning the spade in his rush to escape.

Jan’s stomach dropped. “What’s wrong?”

“It’s not a fox, it’s—”

Her husband screamed. Bone crunched out of sight and his legs kicked with agony. Jan froze for a moment in shock. Fighting inertia, she grabbed one of his feet and hauled backward without success. Something was holding onto the other end of her husband, something insanely strong.

Greg screamed again, begging for help through a wail of terror and pain. Jan lost her grip and fell on her arse as her husband was tugged under the hedge. She howled, tears flooding her face.

An awful rip of flesh assaulted her ears and her husband fell silent. Hairs rose on the back of Jan’s neck, primeval senses warning a killer had turned its attention to her. Dry leaves crunched under paw as the predator crept forward.

Jan crawled to her knees as a broad snout emerged from the greenery. The beast locked bloodshot eyes onto her, lips withdrawn in a snarling rictus. Jan lurched to her feet and ran for the house, fear stealing her voice. Branches slapped as the creature burst from the hedge in pursuit.

Jan pushed herself, demanding speed from a rotund body that hadn't exceeded a brisk walk in thirty years. Paws slapped the ground behind, panting so close she could almost feel it on her neck. She knew she wasn't going to make the door, not with fifty paces still separating the two of them.

Jan snatched a bamboo stake from a vegie patch and turned to face her hunter, breath wheezing between her lips. It sprinted toward her, blood streaming from a scalp laceration where Greg had hit it with the spade. It crashed into Jan's chest, knocking her to the ground. Winded, her mouth gaped as the creature lunged, taking her face in its jaws.

CHAPTER SIX

Carter thanked the barista, picked up his takeaway coffee and walked from a visitor centre perched at the top of the slope, down into Port Arthur's grounds. He found a bench to sit and sipped his cappuccino, content to take in the scenery before starting the task Rylan had set him to survey the numbers of a cryptid known to inhabit the site.

A series of ancient sandstone buildings clustered the edge of a sheltered bay. Most lacked a roof, only the outer shell of yellow stone remaining, however, a few stood intact after all these years. Built as a penal colony and prison, between 1830-1877, Port Arthur had housed the most hardened of British criminals, men and women who were secondary offenders upon arrival in Australia, or who had rebelled whilst in other convict stations. Prisoners in the colony were put to work, cutting timber from the surrounding bush or working in the shipyard. Punishments on site had been common, from floggings to lengthy stints in solitary confinement.

Port Arthur had eventually become a tourist attraction, visitors travelling from far and wide to appreciate the stark beauty of the old buildings and eery setting. But in 1995, evil had returned in the form of a lone gunman. For no known reason, Martin Bryant murdered thirty-five men, women and children in cold blood, and wounded another twenty-three. The killer had hunted adults and children alike through buildings and about the carpark, shooting so many in the park's small cafe that it had been demolished to expunge the stain.

Port Arthur's beauty was sullied by the death and misery saturating its land, the morbid history sinking into the earth like blood, creating a cold sensation that had nothing to do with the weather. Carter closed his eyes and emptied his mind. He concentrated on the sounds around him, the feeling of the breeze on his skin, the slight fluctuations in temperature. Before entering the Cryptid Investigation Unit, Carter would have ignored any sensation he couldn't rationally explain, but not anymore. He'd seen enough to question his old beliefs, from paranormal entities to beasts ripped from myth and legend. Another shiver worked up his spine, hairs standing along his arms like tiny sentinels of warning. Emotion had stained the land of Port Arthur; terror, hatred, and misery experienced to such an extent that it would never be cleansed.

Carter looked toward a bare concrete slab, all that remained of the demolished café, and made a mental note to stay clear. After so much violent death, ghosts would be stuck in limbo, reliving their last moments of terror, confusion and pain. Not all people felt their presence, but for Carter, walking across those foundations would be like plunging into a pool of icy water. He watched as a family of three passed over its surface. Mother and child were oblivious, but the father stopped and shivered, tightening his coat as he looked over his shoulder with a confused frown of trepidation.

Carter upended the last of his coffee, threw it in a bin and stood. He had work to do. Places such as Port Arthur attracted an interesting class of cryptid, beasts that fed on emotion and sadness. Chameleon in nature, they were extremely difficult to find, their skin reflecting light in a range invisible to the human eye. Known by the uncomplimentary name 'bin-scab', the species was commonly found in urban parks frequented by the homeless. Feeding off the distress of humans suffering poor mental health, drug addiction, or the indignity of being ignored and abandoned by wider society, bin-scabs were often harmless. However, if allowed to congregate in excessive numbers they could become a menace.

Carter debated for a moment where he would be most likely to find the beasts. The foundations of the demolished cafe was a likely target, however the area was too open, giving the cryptids little cover to hide. He turned around and settled on the solitary confinement cells of the Separate Prison. Housing those who had broken rules within the prison itself, convicts had been locked in cells without light and sound for up to a month, sending many of them insane.

A short walk brought him inside the building. Oppressively small cells lined each side of the hall. Barely large enough for a man to lie down, cold emanated from the whitewashed cell walls, leaching heat from even the few sunlit areas. A light sensation closed about Carter's throat, a nauseating claustrophobia at the thought of being stuck in one of these rooms, alone with the demons of his mind.

A group of tourists crowded the far end of the hall, each wearing orange headphones of a self-directed tour. He waited for them to move on, then walked to the front of a cell. Carter stood on his tiptoes and peered through a small viewing hole in the door that would have been used by the guards. The cell was deep in shadow, a simple cloth mattress on the floor to one side, demonstrating how it would have been furnished. As he stared, a sense of coolness brushed over his ear and down his neck. Carter paused, determining from which direction the feeling was strongest.

Above, a handspan to the right.

Without looking, he stabbed a hand up with fingers splayed. Instead of hitting stone, his fingers closed on something slick and cold above the door's lintel, like gripping a raw sausage straight from the fridge. The cryptid whipped in his grasp, and he threw up his other hand to maintain his hold. Carter tore the beast from its haunt and dropped to the floor. Using his knees and one hand to keep it in place, he fished a small jar of chalk powder from his jacket pocket. Teeth gritted with effort, he awkwardly unscrewed the jar and shook out some of the dust. The chalk settled over the cryptid, making it visible for the first time. Like a giant axolotl, the beast was devoid of hair, with a wide shovel of a head and four legs.

It twisted and snapped, displaying a mouth of serrated teeth. The cryptid lunged again, a tooth scraping a sliver of skin from the back of Carter's hand. Mucous oozed from its back and head, washing the white dust from its body in a flood of clear fluid. Having seen enough to describe the species accurately, Carter released his grip and jumped back. Near invisible again, the creature ran for the shadows further down the hall.

Carter picked up the chalk container, screwed the lid back on and stowed it in his pocket, grinning. Seeing an animal that few others even knew existed gave him a buzz, and the fact it was the first cryptid species he'd found without any help from Rylan made it even more satisfying.

He brushed off his hands, patted chalk dust from his clothes and made for the exit. A cloud crossed the sun as he clumped down some steps to the road, dropping the temperature perceptibly. Taking a woollen beanie from his pocket, he pulled it down over his ears, blocking out the cold. He turned on the spot, boots crunching on gravel as he looked for another spot to search.

***

Anton led them to a new building outside. Shaped somewhat like a plane hangar, walls of gunmetal-grey soared six metres to an arched roof. The front half of the building was enclosed by plexiglass, the rear by wire mesh to let in the weather. Rylan eyed the security guard standing at the entrance. He stepped forward to block Marat and Rylan's entrance.

"Please hand over your phones and any video or sound recording equipment." The guard held out an open-topped box and waited.

Anton shrugged his shoulders and gave a sheepish smile. "What you're about to see is highly confidential. We have strict protocols to ensure it stays that way until we're ready to go public."

Rylan handed over her phone without fuss, but Marat was less than happy, grumbling under his breath. The guard locked both phones in a small safe by the entrance.

"Excellent, let's enter, shall we?"

Rylan watched Anton type in a six-digit code, out of habit taking note of the numbers entered by his hand movements. A green light glowed above the pad, followed by a click as the door unlocked. Anton swung it open and waved his guests forward.

"Welcome to the nursery, where our thylacine joeys live once they've outgrown the foster parent's pouch."

Rylan stared around the open area in quiet amazement. At least one hundred metres long by fifty wide, the building enclosed a near perfect replica of the outside bushland, all kept green and alive by huge overhead lights and sprinklers. The trio stood on a raised walkway that hugged the outer wall. Three metres below, a fern twitched.

Rylan walked to the handrail and peered down as a young thylacine pushed into the open. Roughly the size of a Jack Russel terrier, it raised a nose to sniff the air. Dark stripes crossed its spine, interspersed by sandy-coloured hair.

"We have fifteen joeys in total. During the day, they usually sleep in a den at the far end. However, we skipped their usual feeding period last night in the hope they'd be more active today.

"While protected from the outside world, we teach skills they'll need to survive in the wild." Anton stepped between his guests and leaned on the railing with both hands. "Starting with butchered pieces of meat, we graduated them onto less prepared cuts and eventually whole carcasses to scavenge. The next step was a little more challenging, but also exciting."

Anton grabbed two whistles and a laser pointer from a peg on the wall behind.

"Before feeding, we gain their attention with this whistle," explained Anton, before blowing a short sharp note. "The joeys recognise this as a notification that an order is soon to follow. In this instance, it's telling them a hunt is about to start." Anton pressed a button on the wall. An electronic motor kicked into action below, and suddenly a streak of grey erupted from a hole in the wall at ground level. Rylan tracked its movement, quickly realising it was an artificial rabbit on a wire.

"Our thylacines must be able to acquire their own food, and it's up to us to not only instil the skills but show them which animals they should pursue. Although there's a rabbit on today's wire, we interchange the prey with other targets that will eventually make up their diet. Animals such as the kangaroo, wallaby and various rodents take a turn on the wire. We hope they will also play a part in reducing feral cat and dog populations."

Anton aimed the laser pointer so that a red dot appeared on the rabbit's back for a short time.

"We use the laser to signify the moving bait as prey, and then encourage them to attack with this last whistle." Anton raised the second whistle to his lips and blasted a high-pitched noise that clawed at Rylan's eardrums.

As the rabbit was dragged through the undergrowth, several joeys erupted from cover in pursuit. Soon there were ten in motion, lithe bodies threading between the plants at speed, attacking as a pack. Two broke from the group, anticipating the established path of the rabbit before the wire turned. The leading animal of the pair leapt at the approaching rabbit, teeth closing around the creature's neck and snatching it from the line. The rest of the pack converged, yips and snarls as they fought over the prize. Blood spattered as the rabbit was torn apart and consumed.

Rylan turned to Anton. "Was that a real animal on the lure?"

Anton shrugged. "Euthanised beforehand, of course. If it was a scrap of material, they'd quickly lose interest."

Rylan grimaced and looked down at the pack, intrigued by the degree of cooperation displayed. When she'd hunted thylacines a century before, she'd never seen more than a family unit together.

"Unlike wolves and dogs, thylacines aren't pack animals. They hunted alone, or at most, in pairs. Are you concerned about fostering unnatural habits?"

Anton's cheeks flushed. "I assure you, Ms Rylan, we have made every effort to remain faithful to the thylacine's true behaviours. But no program can perfectly replicate the teaching process of an adult to its joey."

Unperturbed by the researcher's curt tone, Rylan stared down at a juvenile. The creature sat on its haunches, licking a paw before using it to wipe at blood on its face, an action akin to feline cleaning behaviour. And there was something else about the animal that didn't seem quite right. Her gaze traced from the tail, over the back and up to the head. The joey raised its snout and yawned, jaw hinging wide to display a fearsome collection of canines.

It's the head.

"Why are their skulls so broad? Aside from the snout, these specimens have boxy heads reminiscent of a pit bull… no, a mountain lion. I recall them looking different."

"You *recall*?" laughed Marat, mockingly. "Come now, these animals have been extinct for a century. No one alive today could claim such a thing. I believe you are being unnecessarily harsh on Naturtech's achievements."

Rylan clenched her teeth briefly in irritation. "Yes, I *recall,* Marat. Thylacines are faithfully rendered in many photos, and there's even video footage of the last creature kept at Hobart Zoo."

"Come now, Marat, Ms Rylan has a keen eye and valid point. I was initially worried about the same thing before remembering the vast majority of those photos depict adults. These, however, are *juveniles*. I expect their dimensions will gradually morph until they match the adult form with which we're familiar." He turned to Rylan and presented a somewhat strained grin. "Think of the papers we'll publish in the future, detailing the growth and life cycle of the Tasmanian thylacine. We have so much to learn!

"Now, we must leave these youngsters in peace after their hunt." Anton ushered them both outside, taking care to lock the door.

The security guard took his time retrieving their phones, handing them over with a sullen expression before retreating to his post and picking back up a ragged paperback. Rylan pitied the man. She'd completed her fair share of sentry duty over the years, and there was nothing more boring than standing guard for hours on end.

"Unfortunately, this is where our tour finishes. I appreciate your time, and hope I've demonstrated your financial commitment to Naturtech is reaping dividends."

Rylan accepted Anton's handshake as the guard spoke into his radio, calling a Jeep to their location. "When do you plan on making a public announcement? Such news will attract millions in funding."

"I don't want to jump the gun, Ms Rylan. My aim's to first have our beauties breeding independently and ready for release. When the cameras come for the first time, I want them to see a species in all its glory, adults in their prime."

Rylan gave a slight nod, letting the topic drop. She would raise it again later in private, along with other points of concern. A Jeep pulled up beside her. The guard driving it walked around and opened the passenger door.

"I'll give you a lift to your car, ma'am."

Rylan glanced across at Marat. "I'm happy to wait if you would like to take Mr Drakar first. There's a few topics I want to discuss with Anton."

"I'm so sorry, Ms Rylan, but that will have to wait for another day. Marat is due to fly out shortly, so this is my only opportunity for him to sign some documents in person. I hope you don't mind," said Anton.

Annoyed at the dismissal, Rylan climbed into the vehicle, allowing the guard to close the door behind her. As the Jeep drove off, she glanced behind to see Marat staring after her with a stony expression. Suddenly, the guard swerved to the edge of the road and stopped, making way for an oncoming truck. Of an odd design, the truck had enclosed cages fastened to the tray, pens of a sort to transport greyhounds, but on a much larger scale.

Rylan frowned as the guard proceeded to the exit. She was pleased to see the species resurrected, but there were far too many questions raised by her visit. Questions that one way or another, would be answered.

CHAPTER SEVEN

"What the fuck, Anton?" growled Marat. "I've paid tens of thousands of dollars upgrading security to protect this project, and you go and *invite* an outsider to view the lot?"

Anton winced. He'd known Marat would be pissed, but he'd seen little option.

"There was no other way. Sophia Rylan's the founder of Naturtech. She set up the original foundation with a massive grant, provided the labs, hardware and even wrote some of the software we use. That being said, her supervision of the project is minimal. If I feed her believable crumbs of information, she's happy to leave us alone. But she's no pushover. If I become obstructive, I risk her searching for answers herself."

Marat's face darkened. He closed space and grabbed Anton by his shirt. "How long had you planned to keep this information from me?"

"Naturtech existed before you arrived. Research institutes like us don't exist without financial backers," said Anton, doing his best to keep his voice steady. "I expected a business such as Scarpoint would have completed independent investigations. If you're blindsided by Rylan's involvement, it's down to the sloppy work of your employees."

"Watch it, little man," growled Marat. He twisted his grip, tightening the material around Anton's neck until his face flushed pink. "Do not overstep your position. I *own* you now." Marat released his hold and shoved the manager away. Anton rubbed at his throat, fear battling with anger on his face.

"You said Ms Rylan wrote some of your software? Does she retain access to your computer systems?"

Anton took a step back, making sure he was out of arm's reach. "I don't think so, but it may be possible. I'd have to get our IT guy to check."

"Sort it out. If she becomes a problem, Ms Rylan will find her days numbered." Marat turned away, looking toward another building past the juveniles' enclosure. "Time is moving on. Where are the adult thylacines? You said you had a pack ready for service?"

Anton straightened, happy to change the topic. He extracted a small tablet computer from inside his jacket and turned on the screen. "I believe our adult thylacines fulfill your specs perfectly." Anton showed Marat the screen, displaying an animation of the resurrected species in full flight. "Scarpoint sought a biological weapon, one that could be denied as a deep fake if captured on video. And now you have it. A previously extinct hunter, ready to dispatch against your enemies."

Marat took the tablet from Anton, his eyes hungrily absorbing the displayed stats. "Does it have the characteristics we wanted?"

Anton nodded. "They're proven killers, each and every one. You wanted strength, ferociousness, and the ability to hunt and cooperate as a pack. We have achieved it all."

Anton retrieved the tablet and walked Marat to the next building. “I’m proud of our graphics, but they don’t do justice to the actual creatures.”

This time, the stationed guard made no effort to take phones or obstruct their path, merely stepping aside with a nod. Anton entered his code and pushed open the door to a stairwell. He flicked on a light and led Marat down a flight of carpeted stairs.

Anton looked over his shoulder as they descended. “At this time of day, we’ll find them sleeping. There’s little information on the type of den habited by thylacines in the wild, however we thought it likely they utilised burrows created by wombats, altering them somewhat for their own use.”

Anton opened a second door at the base of the stairs, leading Marat into a dimly lit, narrow room. A long pane of one-way glass filled a wall, giving visual access to the thylacine den. Below the glass was a narrow table with chairs where observers could take notes and record behaviour.

“We created this den for them, however within a week, they enlarged the sleeping chamber seen behind the glass and dug a separate access tunnel.”

Marat walked up to the window until he stood with his nose almost against it. Several adult thylacines slept on the other side, snuggled together for warmth in a misshapen tangle of fur and legs.

“They’re bigger than I expected,” grunted Marat, with approval.

Anton exhaled a quiet sigh of relief, noting the improved expression of the mercenary.

“I take it you were able to use the DNA samples I procured? They cost me a pretty penny; what was so important they be added?” asked Marat.

“Although somewhat impressive, the true thylacine was actually reticent around humans, preferring to retreat where possible. They were also smallish in stature, no bigger than a border collie. The additional genetic information was crucial to change the thylacine’s nature and physical features to fit your needs.”

Anton extracted his tablet again, quickly tapping away at the screen to bring up two pictures, one of a strange type of lion, the other a more recognisable species of canid.

“We spliced DNA from an extinct Australian predator, the thylacocleo carnifex, to increase its size and bite force. A type of marsupial lion, thylacoleo carnifex is the largest carnivore in Australia’s history. Owning fearsome canines and a monumental bite force, it hunted giant megafauna through Australian forests of the last ice age.

“And to add an instinct for pack cooperation and stamina, we inserted various genes from the modern African wild dog. Hunting in packs of up to forty individuals and able to run at speeds of up to seventy kilometres per hour for hours on end, it’s little wonder that the wild dog is the most successful hunter of the African plains, achieving kills in 85% of their attacks.”

Marat raised a hand and tapped at the one-way glass.

“Please don’t do that. They’ve shown no awareness of this observation post; I’d prefer to keep it that way.”

The Scarpoint mercenary ignored him, tapping louder. "Wake up, little doggies. I want to see how tall you are."

An ear twitched within the sleeping pack, and suddenly a wide head popped up. Its ears swivelled back and forth, searching for the noise that had awoken it. The thylacine yawned, the lower jaw unhinging to an impressive ninety degrees, displaying a milky-white set of canines and cutting teeth. It extracted itself from its siblings and stretched, thigh muscles trembling as it yawned again. Standing to waist height on an adult human, the beast was impressively built. Matching the bite strength of an African lion, it had a broad skull that tapered into a wider than normal snout of a dog. Shoulders and hind legs were heavily muscled, individual groups moving under the short hair like that of an elite race-horse.

"My god, but you're a beauty," said Marat. He rapped the glass with his knuckles, harder this time. "Come over here, my pretty, give me a closer look."

At the loud noise, any semblance of calm left the creature. Its head flicked toward the glass, tail and body stiffening as it sniffed the air. Anton knew it was impossible for the thylacine to see through it, but for the life of him, he could have sworn it stared straight into his eyes. A note of fear squirmed through his gut. He'd seen the beasts in action and had no desire to be the focus of their hunger.

"Come now, Marat, I said to not disturb the animals in the den…"

"Shut up, Anton." The merc knocked on the glass. "Come 'ere, bitch."

The thylacine leapt. Clearing three metres in a split second, it crunched into the glass with jaws spread. The whole pane shook with the impact, a dull crack sounding from somewhere in the structure. Anton pulled Marat back, the mercenary laughing with excitement as the beast scrabbled at the window with its front paws, barking wildly.

"I don't think your beasty is a stupid as you think," said Marat. "It knows something is back here."

Anton stifled the insult on his lips, instead focused on steering Marat back to the stairwell. "No, they're not dumb by any standard. Throughout training, they've constantly surprised us by how quickly they learn and adapt. To tell the truth, it's been a challenge to stay one step in front of them and maintain control over the pack."

Marat walked up the stairs with a new sense of energy in his step. "Then I believe it's time to test their capability, no?"

Anton followed him out into the afternoon light, squinting after the gloom of the observation room. "I don't get what you mean. What test did you have in mind?"

Marat paused, casting a sardonic look his way. "You play the fool poorly, my friend. Are they ready or not?"

Anton swallowed nervously, a sick feeling in his stomach as he nodded.

"Good. Then have their trainer bring them into the open. I want to see them in action."

***

Anton watched as a black van reversed to the edge of the enclosure. Windows at the back of the vehicle were blacked out, obscuring the interior. As the dust settled, the rear door popped open and a Scarpoint soldier jumped down onto the dirt, joined soon by the van's driver. The two men dragged a bound and gagged man from the back, dumping him unceremoniously on the ground. The man was unkept, his clothes unwashed and filthy. A patchy grey beard sprouted from his jawline, framing a face thick with grime and spattered with open sores. He strained at his ties, eyes staring fearfully around.

Marat had insisted the thylacines be blooded with their first human kill, and yet, Anton was nevertheless stunned to see an actual man trussed and ready for sacrifice. He stuffed a hand in his pocket and pinched his thigh through the material. No, this wasn't a dream.

"Did you eat something bad for lunch, Anton?" laughed Marat. "You look like you're about to be sick."

"I'm fine," said Anton. Although the merc wasn't far off the truth, he wasn't about to admit it. Anton swallowed an acid taste and cleared his throat. "Who is he?"

Marat shrugged. "No one that will be missed. We found him sleeping on the streets, unconscious with an empty bottle of cheap whiskey. I'd say any family gave up on him decades ago."

Marat gestured at one of his workers. "Get him ready."

Anton watched as the guards cut the ties about the homeless man's limbs and pulled him to his feet. The man started yelling around the gag and struggling until one of the guards punched him hard, a cheek bone audibly crunching beneath his fist. The homeless man slumped, and they dragged him toward the enclosure.

Anton lurched into motion. His limbs felt odd, like there was a delay between thought and action as he approached the gate. Anton punched his code and the gate buzzed, a small green light blinking as the lock sprung open. One of the guards nudged the gate aside, then shoved the victim inside. He stumbled, managing one step before falling flat on his face. After a moment, he struggled to his feet again, blood streaming from his nose in a sheen of crimson. Now that he had his hands free, he ripped the gag from his mouth.

"Let me out of here, ya fuckin' cunts!"

"You Australians," said Marat with a bemused expression. "Speak so eloquently, I could listen to it for hours. Alas, we have work to do. Bring our beauties out to play, Anton."

"I said, let me OUT! I have fuckin' rights!"

Anton pulled a remote control from his jacket and swallowed his nervousness. "We have amalgamated the different whistles and laser pointers used to guide the animals into this one device."

He pushed a button at the top and looked to the side expectantly. A panel slid aside in the wall with an electric buzz, opening a passage down to the den. Within moments, adult thylacines trotted into the open, eyes squinting at the change in light.

The homeless man backed away, grabbed the locked gate and began to shake it violently. He looked over his shoulder at the beasts, eyes wide with fear. “Get me out of here! Please, I’ll do *anything*.”

Anton forced himself to ignore the man. *De-personalise the situation. He’s not a human, just bait in a training exercise.* Before the thylacines decided to attack on their own volition, he pressed another button on the control, causing it to emit a high tone. In response, the thylacines sat on the ground, their faces turning to him expectantly. Anton pressed another button, and a red laser dot appeared on the homeless man’s chest. The pack responded to the instruction, locking their attention upon the terrified man.

Marat grinned at the victim. “They look a little hungry. I hear there’s another way out of the enclosure in that direction,” he said, pointing south along the fence line. “I suggest you run.”

The man gave the gate a one last shake of desperation, eyes wide as he glanced over his shoulder at the thylacines. He snorted, then hocked a gob of green sputum at Marat’s feet, a last futile act of defiance before he gave in and ran. Disgust battled with pity in Anton’s eyes as he watched. Years of drugs and alcohol had robbed the man of any athletic ability, his gait shambling and barely coordinated enough to stay upright.

“That’s enough of a head start. Order them to attack.” Marat’s face was flushed, pupils dilated with excitement.

Anton depressed a button on his controller, emitting the high-pitched attack whistle that always put his teeth on edge. The pack leapt into pursuit, yips and barks sounding between them. Within ten metres the pack spread out, two animals sprinting ahead to get in front of the drunk and close off his line of escape. The man had no chance. They caught him in mere seconds, the lead thylacine knocking him to the ground in a tangle of limbs. Once on the ground, his death was brutally fast, throat torn out in a spray of blood. The beasts began to feed even as his legs drummed the dirt.

Anton turned his gaze aside, not wanting to watch the animals feast. Sensing they had eaten enough to respond to commands, he pressed another button, a calming whistle of recall. At this sound, the pack disengaged from the corpse, trotting back to their den. Gore drenched their jaws and chest as they passed the watching Scarpoint leader.

Marat walked over to Anton and held out his hand for the control. Somewhat reluctantly, Anton handed it over.

"Now *that* is a neat device," said Marat, turning it over in his hand. "Can the volume be increased?"

"I don't think so," said Anton, an eyebrow raised in question. "Can I ask why?"

"Firearms tend to make our work environment a little noisy. I need our thylacines to hear their orders whatever the situation."

"I'll get my engineer to add the function," said Anton. "Now, while you have the controller in hand, there are a few things to show. It is early days, so the commands are limited to basic instructions. Simple stuff like, stay, attack, return."

"And if I lose the controller?"

Anton took a slow breath, looking over to the mangled corpse. "Then your only means to direct their behaviour is gone. I would strongly encourage you *not* to lose it."

CHAPTER EIGHT

Two coffees in hand, Carter dodged around tourists in the Port Arthur visitor centre and made for a small table where his partner waited. Outside the windows, darkness crept over the ruins with the fall of night. Rylan glanced up and accepted the offered cup with a nod of thanks.

"I'm kind of surprised you went for the ghost-tour idea," said Carter, taking a seat. "I could have dropped you back to the hotel."

"Hey, if we see something, it'll be a bonus," said Rylan with a shrug. "But it's not why I came."

Carter raised an eyebrow in question.

"That creature you found in the isolation cells, it wasn't a bin-scab, nor does it fit the description of an Australian native."

"You think it's an invasive species?"

Rylan nodded. "I'm almost certain it was a grief-sucker. They infest the jails of Mexico City, feeding on misery and sometimes the prisoners. Many murders attributed to gang killings are actually the work of those nasty beasts. Get one angry enough, and it'll go on a rampage."

Carter swallowed, thankful now that he'd escaped his first encounter with barely a scratch. "Central America's half a world away. Did it catch a ride on a container ship or something?"

"Maybe, but this would be the third occurrence in two years. I think they're being imported," said Rylan.

"Come on, surely there's not a market for things like this?"

"You'd be surprised. I could name several cryptid enthusiasts off the top of my head, people with obscene levels of wealth who would pay millions for a rare specimen. But acquiring a cryptid's often easier than keeping it. Few know how to care for the rarer beasts, so they commonly die or escape."

"Okay, but the grief-sucker was near invisible, I only found it through dumb luck. How do you plan on finding another?"

"Tetrochromia."

Carter just gave her a flat stare. "Ah, you're going to have to expand on that."

"It's an eye condition I have. Basically, I see a wider spectrum of colours than the average person. To my eyes, the mucous oozed by grief-suckers lights up like purple neon."

Of course it does. Next thing, I'll find out she can read minds. "That must come in handy."

"For finding cryptids, yes. But in general life, not so much."

"How so?"

"For one thing, hotel rooms light up like a Jackson-Pollock of human fluids."

Carter nearly choked on a mouthful of coffee, half of it going down the wrong way. "You mean, you can see…" He broke off, coughing.

"Yes," said Rylan with a lip-curl of revulsion. "All I can say is, never sleep with the bedspread. Those things are never washed."

Carter grimaced. "Ah, on a different topic, how did your meeting go? You mentioned Naturtech had a research breakthrough?"

"Yeah, it was more than significant." Rylan bit her lip, looking like she was debating how much to tell him. Until now, she'd kept her life outside of the Cryptid Investigation Unit completely separate from work.

"I've been involved with Naturtech since it was just an idea." Rylan leaned back and gave Carter an overview of the company, its origins, research programs and recent achievements. "I've got enough on my plate at the CIU and I fucking hate micro-managers, so until now, I've allowed the people I employed to get on with their job. Unfortunately, it seems the freedom I granted the general manger has come at a cost." Rylan frowned. "If my concerns are right, I might need to cancel the whole research program before more harm is done."

Carter put down his coffee. "What's wrong with the animal?"

"The morphology is all wrong, and on top of that, Naturtech has secured Scarpoint Industries as a silent partner."

"The private military company? I had the misfortune of working with them in Afghanistan," said Carter. "Ethics weren't high on their priority list. Why would Scarpoint have an interest in this type of research?"

"My question exactly," agreed Rylan. She looked back at her computer, eyes tracking the screen as her fingers flew over the keyboard. "When I set up Naturtech's IT system, I maintained the ability to access their database. I think it's time I searched for a few answers."

Carter sat back, giving her silence to work. A mercenary army and resurrected beasts? Had these bastards not seen Jurassic Park?

"What the f..." Rylan stared up at him over her laptop screen. "They've added DNA from two different species. Some from an ancient marsupial lion called Thylacoleo, alongside canid genes from the African wild dog. Those dumb motherfuckers! No ethicist would condone this research, let alone release such a hybrid into the wild. The damn thing shouldn't even exist!"

Carter had seen African wild dogs in action while travelling through the Laikipia Plateau of Central Kenya. Ignoring his game truck, a pack of sixteen had taken down a wildebeest. The level of teamwork and intelligence displayed by the dogs to kill a much larger creature had been truly amazing.

"Bloody hell, there's more," said Rylan. "The joeys I saw were only a few months old, but I just found reference to live specimens birthed over a year ago. *Fourteen* of the damn things. They'd be adults by now."

"You'd have to wonder why he's kept you out of the loop, boss."

Rylan grunted an agreement, a deep groove carved in her forehead as she concentrated. Suddenly she slammed the screen shut on the laptop, swearing under her breath. "The prick's just locked me out of the system. They know I'm snooping."

"Did you find Scarpoint's angle?" asked Carter.

Rylan shook her head. "No, and that leaves one option."

Carter grinned. "Sounds like we need to pay Naturtech a visit—"

A gut churning scream stunned all to silence. Carter spun in his seat, automatically pinpointing the sound's origin. "That came from somewhere near the old penitentiary."

Rylan was already on her feet, Glock in hand. Another scream sounded, a cry of agony and terror. The noise seemed to break the spell and suddenly the foyer erupted. Some called for the police, others ran for their cars in panic, overturning chairs and shoving tables aside in their haste to leave. Port Arthur had already claimed tens of lives through a gunman's rampage, and no-one wanted to be around for a re-enactment. But as others retreated, Rylan and Carter pushed against the tide and ran toward danger.

"Make way!" Carter held his ID badge in one hand, Glock in the other. "Federal agents, move aside!"

He shouldered aside a door and ran into the park grounds with Rylan close on his tail. Carter followed his ears, running toward the sounds of a slaughterhouse. People sprinted past them in the opposite direction, faces pale and eyes wide with horror. Carter and Rylan bolted through pools of light cast by lamps above, shadows hiding much of the surrounding area. They neared the penitentiary, the large building looming from the darkness like a bruise on the night sky.

Carter scanned the terrain ahead for combatants to engage, effortlessly slipping into habits ingrained through two decades of military service. Carter skidded to a halt with his Glock in a two-hand grip.

It can't be...

A huge thylacine stood over a man, toying with him. Shaped like a gargantuan short-haired wolf, the beast stood taller than Carter's waist, shoulders broad and striped in the unmistakeable black bands of the Tasmanian tiger. The man crawled to his knees, groaning. Blood streamed from multiple wounds, ragged bite marks oozing as the man staggered to his feet and tried to run. The beast allowed him to get two steps before bringing him down again.

Carter lined up a shot, but the civilian blocked his aim, punching feebly at the beast's head. Instead of backing off, the thylacine lunged forward, clamping its jaw about the man's neck. It gave a violent twist, snapping the cervical vertebrae like a piece of timber. The beast dropped its prize and dipped its head to lap at the blood.

Rylan skidded to a halt behind him, heels crunching in the gravel. The thylacine looked up at the noise, just as Carter squeezed off a shot. Instead of burying deep in the creature's head, the round tore a furrow of tissue from its shoulder. It yelped and darted away. Two bounds and it leapt onto the corrugated-iron veranda of an adjacent building, a vertical jump of near two-and-a-half meters. Metal creaked as it bounded over the roof and out of sight.

Rylan growled with irritation. "We split, meet at the back."

Carter nodded and broke left as Rylan went in the opposite direction. A garden of box hedge and roses framed the south side of the building, forcing him wider onto the grass. Recent rain had soaked the area, and within a few steps, the ends of his pants were drenched. Noise from the roof ceased, leaving nothing but the gentle moan of the sea breeze. He slowed, taking advantage of the soft ground to muffle his steps.

The lit path was now far behind him, and it quickly became harder to see. Carter kept his gaze on the roof, searching for any unnatural undulation to suggest a crouched animal in waiting. Carter reached the rear of the building as his boss rounded the far side.

“Did you see anything?”

Rylan shook her head. “It has to be near, though. Maybe it jumped to the next building?”

“Or back onto the ground,” said Carter.

A low growl confirmed his suspicion, the sound deep and guttural. Hairs rose on the back of his neck and Carter spun to the noise. The beast crouched in the garden a few paces away, striped coat blending with the shadows. Carter brought his gun to bear as it launched, muscled legs catapulting the creature at him at amazing speed. He pulled on the trigger twice in haste. The first round missed, the second punched a ragged wound in its belly. The thylacine crashed into him, smashing Carter from his feet and onto his back. He lost his grip on his weapon, the Glock landing out of reach on the grass. Heavy forelimbs with retractable claws pinned him to the ground as Carter fought to dislodge the beast, punching and twisting. The creature’s hindlegs raked his abdomen, claws tearing ribbons from the front of his jacket. The thylacine leant down and growled, spraying warm drops of blood and spit in his face. Its jaw spread wide—

Crack!

The beast was punched to the side, leaving a mist of blood in the air where its head had been. Rylan fired a second round, point blank into the back of its skull to make sure.

Carter climbed to his feet slowly, body awash with the jittery after-effects of adrenaline. He raised his clothes at the front, searching for wounds. Carter had once seen a video of a cornered leopard disembowel a hunter's dog in a similar fashion, tearing through the abdominal musculature to spill the poor creature's guts. He sighed with relief. Aside from a few shallow scratches, his winter jacket had taken the worst of it. If he hadn't been dressed for the Tasmanian winter, it might have been a different story.

Carter collected his Glock and joined Rylan by the creature. She knelt, oblivious to the wet grass, brow furrowed.

"Jesus, they've created a monster. It's near three times the size of a true thylacine. And look at this," she said, picking up a heavy paw. "It has the retractable claws of a thylacoleo."

"Can you imagine if we'd been unarmed?"

Rylan glanced up at him, an eyebrow slightly raised in question. "You'd be dead, get to the point."

"I know you want to right a wrong and bring the Tasmanian tiger back from the grave, but this isn't a true thylacine. It's a freak created in a test tube."

Rylan stood. “I don’t think Naturtech’s breeding them for release. If Scarpoint’s involved, they must be seeking a military use.”

“For the battlefield?”

Rylan nodded. “Why else enhance their predatory abilities unless it serves a purpose? And that leads us to our next problem. When I was leaving Naturtech’s grounds, a truck carrying transport cages arrived.”

Carter groaned. “Tell me you’re kidding.”

“Anton knows I was snooping through their system, so they may try to move the animals quickly. We’ll have to act tonight.”

He nodded in agreement. “We’re going to need more than a Glock to take on a squad of mercs, not to mention their pack of war dogs.”

“Unless you can magic a rifle from thin air, we don’t have much—” Rylan stopped mid-sentence. “That grief sucker, where did you find it again?”

“The solitary confinement cells, why?”

Rylan grinned. “If Scarpoint’s weaponizing a beast, might be time we had one of our own.” She looked down at her watch and swore. “We need to get moving.”

CHAPTER NINE

Sophia Rylan.

Marat knew he'd come across the name, but the question was where? Was she an asset or a target? Scarpoint had grown exponentially over the past twenty years. Legitimate wartime activities were only the tip of a vast iceberg. Below water level and out of sight, Scarpoint was a gun for hire to the underworld. From money laundering and sex trafficking, all the way through to protecting drug lords and the elimination of rival gangs; if the reimbursement was high enough, Scarpoint had a finger in the pie.

Marat opened his laptop and launched a browser named 'Candle', one of the numerous search engines used to navigate the dark web. A bastion of human depravity, the dark web was a place where any perversion could be met for the right price, and a human's life bartered as a simple commodity.

Let's see if you have a contract on your head.

Marat typed the name of a bounty hunter website. He scrolled the list of targets, eyeing fraudulent businessmen, criminals, rapists and thugs. Some people deserved their coming death, others would be the victims of insurance scams or just the petty vengeance of a cold hearted bastard. Scarpoint left the smaller jobs for others. The sort of contracts his business acquired paid in the millions.

There you are.

Marat allowed himself a small smile of satisfaction as a photo of Rylan popped up with an accompanying contract worth twenty million dollars. He read the number a second time. Such a high bounty meant she was either senior military, intelligence or government, and likely difficult to kill.

Not just a research philanthropist. But none of us ever are.

Marat clicked on the photo, entered his pseudonym and accepted the contract. At odds to the usual sequence of events, a new box appeared on the screen containing a non-disclosure clause and a download button. By reviewing the contract and files, he committed himself to silence, or activated a bounty upon his own head. Marat clicked without a second thought.

Why are you worth so much money?

A series of documents and photos downloaded rapidly, automatically opening as his phone began to vibrate. Marat hit the screen to answer and raised it to his ear.

"Marat Drakar?" asked a digitalised voice.

The Scarpoint officer's lip curled in irritation. "Who is this?"

The voice on the other end of the line ignored his question. "You have accepted a contract for Sophia Rylan. Upon your screen are a series of photos dating back to the mid 1800s—all of the target in question."

Marat swore as his computer became controlled by an outside source, the cursor moving independently, opening different files as the voice spoke on the phone. One photo after another opened and closed. Ms Rylan in a uniform of a Second World War British para-trooper, as a corporal in khaki greens of the First World War, mounted as a trooper of the Light Horse Brigade in the Boer War.

"Is this a joke?" growled Marat. "These photos are doctored. No one can live this long; she'd be over a hundred and forty years old."

"On the contrary. That is precisely the reason a contract exists for Ms Rylan. We have discovered her involvement in military engagements dating back to the late 1700s. Ms Rylan fought in multiple key battles and campaigns under different names. Of note, she secured the rank of Lieutenant Colonel during the Peninsula War of 1807-1814 against the First French Empire, bloodied her sword during the Battle of Waterloo, and somehow emerged unscathed from the charge of the Light Brigade during the Crimean War of 1854.

"Sophia Rylan is an oddity. A human that survives wounds mortal to any other, a human that *re-animates* if killed."

"Oddity?" scoffed Marat. "If that's true, she's no oddity, she's a bloody mutant."

"Mutant, cryptid; call her what you will. In another age, we may have labelled her a god." The digitised voice was flat, emotionless. "But one fact remains, she represents an incredible opportunity for scientific advancement, and a key to achieving eternal life."

Scientific advances, my arse. Marat was no fool. He'd catered to dictators, despots and tyrants across the world, and knew at a glance her true value. She was the perfect fucking soldier, one that couldn't be killed. An army of her like would be invincible.

Placed in the hands of a ruler like Russia's Putin, it would walk across Europe and change the face of the earth.

"Who owns the contract?" asked Marat.

"For the purpose of this transaction, my client has assumed the reference name 'Arctic Fox'."

Marat suppressed a chuckle. *Arctic Fox.* Jacob Freidman, the billionaire owner of the Silver-Trust Corporation, had insisted on using the same ridiculous code name on a previous job where Scarpoint had destroyed the infrastructure of a rival firm.

"When do I get paid?"

"A holding facility has been prepared in the port of Rotterdam. Upon delivery of the cargo, payment will be transferred in full to your nominated account."

"Good. I will notify you once Ms Rylan is in my possession."

Marat closed the lid of his laptop, his mind buzzing with the possibilities a cryptid like Rylan could provide Scarpoint. There was zero chance he would deliver such a prize to Freidman, not until he secured future rights to all military patents developed from her DNA.

Marat opened an encrypted application on his phone. A representation of the earth turned slowly on the screen. Signifying the movement of bugged targets, hundreds of pulsing red dots were scattered across the map, mostly clustered in Europe and the Middle East. Marat zeroed in upon Australia and then the state of Tasmania. A single red dot blinked on the island state, and Marat grinned with satisfaction at its location.

A sharp rap of knuckles sounded from the office doorway. He glanced up to see Anton standing sheepishly, one hand fidgeting at a loose thread of his blazer. Marat frowned in annoyance.

"What now?"

Anton cleared his throat. "I had IT run a scan and found an outside IP address accessing our servers. Rylan must be snooping for information. We've kicked her off our system, however it's unclear what she viewed prior to detection. What do you want to do?"

Marat glanced at his phone and grinned as he saw the pulsing red dot move closer. His trip to Tasmania was becoming a lucrative expedition.

"Let her come and ask questions in person, I would truly welcome it. You see, I have discovered that Ms Rylan has some rather endearing qualities. As such, in addition to the thylacines, I will be taking her with me." Marat turned his phone around so that Anton could see the map and red dot approaching Naturtech's main gate. "But we must move quickly. I attached a tracker to Rylan's coat earlier this afternoon, and it appears she is about to arrive. How long until my thylacines can be loaded onto the truck? I want them transported to the port ASAP."

Anton bit at a fingernail nervously. "I could try to have them loaded within an hour. It'll be their first time in a confined cage, so there's a high risk of agitation."

"An hour?" asked Marat in disbelief. "To load some fucking dogs on a truck? Don't be a fool. You've got twenty minutes."

Anton nodded, eyes wide as he bolted from the door.

CHAPTER TEN

Carter brought the car to a stop and pulled on the parking brake. He climbed from the driver's seat, a light rain beginning to patter as he walked to the back of the car and opened the boot.

Rylan joined him, staring over his shoulder at the hulking mass of dead thylacine. Carter had carried the beast to their car, stowing the corpse mere seconds before the first police responder screeched into the parking area. Officially, the attack would be blamed on a wild dog, with any reports of distinctive markings to be actively discredited.

Two green duffle bags sat on top of the thylacine. The agents took a bag each. Carter held his bag out from his leg, lip curled in dislike as the grief-sucker thrashed for a moment in protest before settling. The creature's mucous had soaked into the material, and Carter had no desire to be coated in the goop.

"That's a little disconcerting," said Rylan. "Those gates were closed and secure today."

Carter slammed the boot and followed his boss's line of sight. A large automatic gate was open and unguarded. "Maybe we're too late. They could have taken the adult thylacines and left?"

"Or our arrival's anticipated." Rylan sighed and made for the opening, leaving Carter to catch up with a few quick strides. "Only one way to find out."

Carter moved the bag to his left hand and drew his Glock. Dense bush encroached the road to either side, tree branches arching above to create a tunnel of sorts. Cold wormed its way down Carter's neck as wind shivered the leaves, bringing the darkness to life. The rain became heavier, fat drops forming puddles in the dirt. Carter wiped water from his brow and flipped up his collar. Lamp posts were spaced at regular distances along the left side of the road, but the two agents avoided the jaundiced pools of light like a disease.

Bush soon gave way to the Naturtech complex. A black truck stood on the road, cabin light on and empty. As they neared the reception building, a flood lamp switched on above its doorway, drowning the area in harsh white light. Carter dropped the duffle bag to take a double-handed grip on his Glock and squinted into the glare, scanning quickly about the road. The door slid aside, and two men stepped out, careful to stay under cover to avoid the rain. One wore a jumper emblazoned with Naturtech's logo, the other a simple black suit.

Rylan took another step forward and raised her ID badge in one hand. "Anton Ricci and Marat Krakar, you're under arrest for crimes in the Criminal Code Act, Part 5.3; producing a weapon that could be used in a terrorist act."

Marat just laughed. "Look at you, a drowned rat giving orders you can't enforce. To be honest, I expected a little more, Ms Rylan."

He lifted his gaze beyond them and gave a nod. Two red dots blinked into life upon each of their chests.

"You see, I have a Scarpoint squad at my disposal. More than enough to deal with you two."

Movement in Carter's peripheral vision drew his attention. Four mercenaries crept from the shadows, laser-sighted rifles trained on the pair. Carter swore under his breath. Marat was right, he had the upper hand for the moment.

"You sure you want to go this way, Marat?" said Rylan. "Using a private military force on Australian land without government approval? I'll see you locked in a federal prison for life."

Carter glanced at his boss from the corner of his eye. She almost sounded bored.

"Well, we can't have that, can we?" said Marat. He hooked a finger at the soldier to Carter's right, any façade of humour disappearing. "Cuff them. If they struggle, shoot to kill."

"Drop your weapon!" shouted the merc, closing aggressively until the rifle barrel touched Carter's forehead.

"All right," muttered Carter, tossing his Glock to the side. "Don't get your knickers in a twist."

"On the ground, NOW!"

Kicked from behind, Carter's knees buckled. A second blow connected with the back of his head, and suddenly he was sprawled on his face, a starburst before his eyes. Carter grunted in pain as one of the bastards knelt on his spine and roughly zip-tied his wrists behind his back. The hard strips of plastic bit deep, edges like a dull knife against his skin. The soldier stood again, allowing Carter to roll onto his side, blinking muddy water from his eyes.

Rylan had survived a little better, keeping her knees despite a scalp wound that sluiced blood. She glared at the soldier holding a rifle in her face as another cuffed her wrists.

The soldiers hauled them to standing and patted each for weapons. Carter kept a straight face as they missed a knife in the top of his boot, before being shoved toward the entrance. A soldier picked up Carter's duffle bag and carried it inside, however Rylan's was missed, left in the shadows at the edge of the road.

The agents were marched through the reception and down a narrow hall into a meeting room with a smartboard. Surrounded by tall-backed wooden chairs, a rectangular table took centre stage, the surface a single massive slab of spotted gum timber. Carter was forced to sit while his wrists were fastened to a strut on the back of the chair. He looked across at Rylan, his boss mouthing at him to wait as her hands were similarly restrained. Job done, the two soldiers left, allowing Marat to enter. He walked to the front of the room and leaned back with crossed arms beside the smartboard.

"Sophia Rylan, I've been thinking about you all day." Marat pushed off the wall. "You see, I *knew* I'd heard your name before, it just took me time to realise where."

He reached out a hand and tapped the smartboard screen, bringing it to life. An ancient black and white photo filled the screen. Three uniformed soldiers wearing the tall shako hats of the 13th Dragoons British Cavalry, stared at the camera. Although her hair was cut short and breasts bound flat under the military jacket, the first soldier was undeniably Sophia Rylan. Marat pointed to a date scribbled in the bottom corner—1854.

“This photo was taken shortly after the charge of the Light Brigade during the Crimean War. A disastrous action that stole the lives of three officers and thirty-eight troopers.” He leaned closer to the screen, staring at Rylan’s face. “The passage of time has been remarkably kind to you.” Marat paused and held up his hand as if counting on his fingers. “Maths was never my strongest gift, but if I’m correct, this photo was taken one hundred and sixty eight years ago, and yet you haven’t aged a day.”

Rylan snorted derisively. “Even children can doctor a photo. This means *nothing*.”

“Well, the owner of the Silver-Trust Corporation is convinced you’ve lived a freakishly long time. So certain in fact, that they’re paying Scarpoint twenty million dollars for your… How should I say it politely? … Ah, your acquisition.” Marat smiled as Rylan’s mask momentarily faltered at the mention of Silver-Trust.

“Jacob Freidman may be convinced, but, I remain a sceptic. As you said, deep fakes are easily created these days, so if I’m to believe you’re some type of immortal being, I will have to see it personally.”

Marat drew a Heckler & Koch P30 pistol from inside his jacket and stepped towards Rylan, aiming at her heart.

“You have to be fucking kidding me,” said Rylan.

“Don’t touch her,” growled Carter.

“Or what are you going to do?” asked Marat, his tone condescending. “Yell at me?”

Carter flexed his arms behind the chair, causing the wood to creak under tension.

"I also know your history, Eoin Carter. As a veteran of the Australian SAS, you look down your nose at me as a mercenary, and yet, your regiment stands accused of Afghan war crimes."

Marat sneered. "You're no better than me, I just don't have delusions of fighting for king and country. Let me ask, would you have fought for free? If your only wage was the satisfaction of serving your country while your family starved for the privilege?"

Carter stared back at him, saying nothing.

"No, I thought not. We all fight for money in the end, the only difference being my wage is larger than yours." Marat shook his head, as if clearing his thoughts. "But enough of that. I have to get my war dogs, I mean, thylacines in transit. Time's a wasting."

Marat raised the Heckler and Koch and squeezed the trigger.

Carter cried out as Rylan's body jerked in the chair. Crimson bloomed from the left side of the chest and she slumped, head lolling forward, torso held in place by her fastened wrists.

Marat leaned forward, peering intently at her corpse. He flicked a glance toward Carter. "How long does it take for her to reanimate?"

Carter clenched his teeth. There was no way he'd tell the man anything. If they were to have a chance at escape, he needed Marat to question the information he'd been given.

"You shot her in the heart," he growled. "Last time I heard, humans need one to live. Congratulations, you sick fuck, you've killed her."

Carter pushed aside his own worry that this time she might be dead for real.

Marat straightened with an expression of resigned disappointment. He looked at his watch and yelled for one of the guards in the hallway. A soldier stepped through the doorway.

"Watch these two. If she fails to wake, we'll sink her body at sea."

CHAPTER ELEVEN

Anton stood roadside, watching as the head keeper, Nick, finished loading another thylacine. It was taking longer than planned, but the keeper refused to hurry, concerned at separating the pack from each other for the first time. Nick returned to the enclosure, picked up a spray bottle and pumped the trigger. A fine mist of liquid puffed onto his chest, coating him in a concoction of calming pheromones. Five adult thylacines paced behind the gate, occasionally emitting low whines or barks, their tails stiff with agitation.

Nick pulled the remote from his pocket and pressed a button. The low tone of a woodwind instrument sounded. Each animal responded, sitting on their haunches before the keeper opened the gate and stepped through. Anton grimaced as he saw Nick's gait waver.

Bloody bastard's been drinking again.

Nick slid a collar about the first animal's neck and walked it out of the enclosure. The hybrid thylacine was huge, shoulders of the creature brushing the base of Nick's chest as he walked alongside. The keeper murmured quietly to the animal as he walked to the truck, gentle words of encouragement to keep it calm.

"Ready to open crate eleven," said Nick.

Anton's gaze skipped to the front of the tray. The crates were welded together as a unit that could be lifted from the truck as one. At the front of the structure was a control panel responsible for opening and locking the individual crates. The soldier who'd been there a few minutes earlier was nowhere to be seen. The leashed thylacine barked and lunged at something unseen in the dark, nearly pulling Nick off his feet.

"Crate eleven, open it now!"

Anton jogged to the truck and hauled himself onto the tray. The control panel was buried in shadow, forcing Anton to squint to read the instructions. Seeing a button with the word 'open' above it, he reached a hand up. Just as he was about to push it, he was wrenched back by his belt. Anton hit the ground with a yelp, his left ankle turning painfully.

The soldier who'd pulled him out of the way climbed up and pressed a different button for the waiting keeper. "The crates are individually numbered. You nearly pressed an emergency release to open all the gates at once," scowled the soldier. "Don't touch our equipment, got it?" Job done, the soldier jumped down and stalked away.

Chagrined, Anton limped back to his original position. He looked at his watch and frowned. "Time to hurry it up, Nick. We're running behind."

The keeper ignored him, mumbling something under his breath as he locked the thylacine into its crate.

Anton took a deep breath, trying in vain to still the anxiety buzzing in his chest. Selling a few animals had been one thing, but taking hostages and killing people? He hadn't signed up for this bullshit.

"How long until they're all boarded?"

Nick turned without meeting his eye and began walking back to the enclosure. Growling under his breath, Anton closed the distance and grabbed his shoulder, forcing him to stop. "Damn it Nick, stop ignoring me! I asked how long until they're ready to leave?"

Alcohol wafted off the keeper, making Anton wince. Nick's face was red with fury as he looked at him. "It takes as long as it fucking takes. These animals haven't been loaded on a truck like this; it's a new experience that might set them off." Nick slapped Anton's hand off his shoulder. "And having you bitching from the sidelines isn't making anything easier."

"Watch it, Nick. Keep talking like that, and you'll be out of a job."

Nick sneered, extracted a small bottle of whiskey from his jacket, unscrewed the cap and took a long pull. He drew a sleeve across his mouth and tucked the bottle away again. "You know what? Fuck your job. After what's gone on here today, I'm out."

Anton's gut clenched. "Not before you finish loading the truck. You *can't* go."

"Do it yourself," muttered Nick.

Gravel crunched behind Anton as one of the mercenaries approached. "We got a problem here?"

Nick paled somewhat, forced to look up at the taller man. "I just resigned. You guys are going to have to load the thylacines yourself."

The soldier grabbed Nick's shirtfront and wrenched him forward. The keeper stumbled and yet the soldier took his body weight with ease, forcing him closer until they were nose to nose.

"Stop fucking around. Load the dogs, or I'll start clipping fingers for motivation."

He shoved the keeper back, hard. Nick's heel caught on a rock, and he fell on his arse. The soldier extracted a pocketknife and unfolded a six-inch blade. "Now, are we good, or are you going to pick a finger to lose?"

Growls sounded from the crates aboard the truck, low and angry as the thylacines watched. Nick slowly got to his feet. "Fine, I'll do it, but you guys need to keep back. Once agitated, their behaviour's unpredictable."

A door slammed. Anton glanced behind to see Marat exit the reception building. He groaned inwardly, wanting the whole night to be finished.

"How long until my dogs are loaded?"

The keeper stalked away to the enclosure, leaving Anton to placate the Scarpoint officer. "Shouldn't be long. Only a few more to transfer."

Marat gave a stiff nod. "Good." He paused, looking back to the reception in thought. "How long have you known Sophia Rylan?"

Anton shrugged. "A few years, I guess. Why?"

"Has she aged in that time?"

"Not obviously," said Anton. "Never seen a wrinkle let alone a grey hair. I just wish I had the same amount of money as her to throw at a plastic surgeon. What are you getting at?"

"The Silver-Trust Corporation are under the impression she's immortal, but I'm beginning to think they were mistaken."

"Huh?"

"You see, I put a bullet in her heart, and she's yet to wake up." Marat made the statement with an air of distracted disappointment, as if he'd just placed a two-dollar bet on a losing horse.

"You *shot* her?" Anton's mouth gaped in shock.

A sharp *crack!* of a discharging handgun echoed inside the building.

Marat turned to the sound, a pistol appearing in his grip with the speed of close-up magic. A glint of excitement lit the man's eye. "Maybe Silver-Trust was right after all." He hooked a finger at one of his soldiers. "Come with me."

***

Carter stared at Rylan, heart hammering as he silently begged her to start breathing. The bullet wound at her chest had stopped bleeding shortly after Marat shot her. He waited for any sign of healing, a tinge of pink to her cheek, the flicker of a pulse at her neck. Carter's breath caught as he finally saw movement. A slight tremor ran through her muscles. Starting at her face, fasciculations worked down her body, tiny muscular contractions moving in a slow wave from head to toe. It was like watching her brain complete a reboot, re-establishing control over the soft tissues to bring the body back online. The fine tremors stilled, and a groan exited Rylan's mouth. Her eyelids flickered open, pupils unfocused. The soldier guarding them flinched like he'd seen a ghost.

"Get her some water, will you?" asked Carter, his voice low and urgent.

The merc looked from Carter back to Rylan again, clearly uncertain what to do.

"Come on, man. She's just been shot in the chest."

The soldier scowled and lowered his rifle. He pulled a canteen from his webbing, unscrewed the lid and inched forward tentatively, as if approaching a sleeping tiger. Rylan's eyes slowly tracked up, fixing on the soldier with lids half closed. Her chest rose in shallow breaths, head lolling forward. The soldier gained confidence and moved closer, squatting in front of her. He reached out and moved aside the bullet hole in her shirt to expose the skin.

His jaw slackened. "It's not possible," he murmured quietly. "There's no wound."

"Is that so?" grated Rylan. She smashed her forehead into the soldier's face, spreading his nose sideways. He dropped with a heavy thud, joints unhinging as one.

Carter strained against his bonds and forced himself to stand. The back of the chair flexed, zip-ties digging into the skin of wrists and ankles. He growled, face red and veins bulging until the chair finally splintered. Crimson flooded from his left wrist where the zip-tie had cut deep. Carter worked the fingers of his hand, relieved to find the digits still moving. Whatever damage had been done, the tendons were intact.

Carter extracted a knife from the soldier's belt. Unfolding the blade, he cut the plastic bindings, then set to freeing his colleague.

"Get a dressing around that wound," said Rylan, eyeing his wrist.

Carter nodded, took a field dressing from the soldier's webbing and awkwardly tied it around his wrist. Rylan stripped the man of weapons, keeping the rifle for herself and passing a handgun to Carter. The merc coughed a bloody clump of phlegm and groggily tried to sit.

"Stay down, sunshine," said Rylan. "You ain't going nowhere."

Carter threw a second bandage to Rylan. She gagged and hog-tied the semi-conscious merc before dragging him behind the desk and out of sight.

"Freeze!"

Carter spun, saw a soldier standing in the doorway and fired a shot above his head in warning. "Get out of here. Next shot's in your head," yelled Carter.

The soldier growled, dropped to a squat and raised his weapon. A rifle fired behind Carter and the soldier toppled backward, a ragged hole in the centre of his face. Rylan lowered the rifle and strode to the doorway, checking for further threats.

"Damn fool," she muttered. "You gave him a chance, and he ignored it."

Carter joined her at the door. "Where to next?"

"There's a gun safe and monitors for the CCTV cameras in the security office. Time to top up our ammunition and get a lay of the land."

Carter nodded. Footfalls echoed in the conference room down the hall. People were coming to investigate the rifle shot and they needed to move.

"That way," said Rylan, pointing to the right. "Security was located on the second floor on the original plans, hopefully it's still there."

The two agents took off at a run. Carter shouldered aside a door to a stairwell then let Rylan pass. Taking two steps at a time, she left the stairwell at the next level and jogged down a hall to the left. A door labelled 'security' terminated the corridor.

Carter tried the handle. Locked. He took a step back, raised his foot and stamped with all his force. The locking mechanism splintered from the doorjamb and the door swung open to crash into the adjacent wall. A series of CCTV monitor screens covered the right wall, displaying footage of the various enclosures, buildings and perimeter. A lounging security officer shot to his feet, hand fumbling for a gun at his waist.

"Don't be an idiot," growled Carter. Striding forward, he shoved the barrel of his stolen pistol in the man's face.

The guard froze, hand dropping away from his side arm. "What's going on?"

Carter disarmed the man and slipped the confiscated pistol into the back of his waistband. "How many soldiers does Scarpoint have on site?"

The guard hesitated for a moment, eyes fixed on the end of Carter's pistol. Rylan flashed a badge. "We're federal agents. Your boss is selling assets to a private army; either cooperate or spend the next decade in jail."

The guard swallowed. "I…I'm not exactly sure. Maybe seven?"

"Where are the adult thylacines?" asked Rylan.

The guard nodded toward CCTV monitors. "Camera four shows their enclosure – there's only four left. The rest have been loaded onto the transport."

"Shit," said Rylan under her breath. "Can you bring the truck on screen?"

The guard nodded and hit a few buttons. A screen to the right flipped its picture, changing to a view outside the reception building. In black-and-white, the head keeper prepared to take another thylacine from the enclosure, a heavy leash in his hand.

Carter turned away from the screen. Time was against them. "What weapons do you have here?" asked Carter. "Any rifles?"

"No, only the Glocks. One for each security guard, and all are signed out of the safe."

"Tranquiliser guns?" asked Rylan. "There's got be a sedation protocol if a thylacine got loose."

The guard glanced toward a locked cupboard. Rylan grabbed him by the collar and dragged him over to it.

"Open it. Now."

The guard scowled but typed a six digit code on a touch pad. A small light blinked green, and the cupboard unlatched with a click. Rylan pushed the guard aside and opened the door. Two rifles were mounted on the back wall, boxes of ammunition and pre-packaged naloxone syringes below. As Rylan grabbed one of the rifles, Carter opened a box, finding a series of small darts inside.

"Be careful, each dart contains a dose of carfentanil large enough to drop an adult thylacine—more than enough to kill a man," warned the guard.

Carter looked at the darts with greater respect. An extremely potent opioid, carfentanil was lethal to humans in the smallest of doses. Ten thousand times stronger than morphine, and one hundred times more potent than its closest cousin, fentanyl, the drug quickly caused a drop in conscious level and respiratory arrest. In the event of overdose, its effects could be reversed with an antagonist medication called naloxone he'd seen in the cupboard.

Footsteps echoed in the corridor outside, rapidly gaining in volume. Scarpoint soldiers would be on them within seconds.

"On your belly." Rylan grabbed the guard's collar and forced him to the ground.

The security guard hit the deck, eyes squeezed shut. Rylan loaded a dart in the rifle and lifted it to her shoulder. The footsteps came to a stop.

"Agents Rylan and Carter," shouted Marat from the corridor. "Surrender and you'll come to no harm, I swear on my honour."

Honour?

The merc had none. If they surrendered, Carter would be dead by morning, and his partner a lab monkey. He glanced about, looking for cover or another exit. There were a few desks and chairs, but nothing to stop a bullet.

They were trapped.

He stared at Rylan, found her gaze calm and stony—the look of a soldier about to breach the parapet and take on the enemy. She'd beat him to the same conclusion. There was only one way out of this room, and it was through the enemy.

Carter drew his pistol and chambered a round.

CHAPTER TWELVE

A familiar buzz coursed through Rylan's chest, energy peaking at the imminent prospect of action. Three centuries of soldiering had seen her fight through some of the worst battles in human memory. There was much she hated of war, but if Rylan was honest, she'd become addicted to the adrenaline rush of combat. It was an admission that made her feel dirty, an embarrassment that she could take pride in her capability as a warrior when it came at the cost of human life.

Marat called out, demanding their surrender a second time. Rylan wanted to spit. She'd rather trust a cobra not to strike. Rylan glanced at Carter and mouthed for him to take cover. He nodded and squatted behind a desk, up against the wall.

Rylan dropped a stapler from a nearby table on the tiled floor, causing a clatter of metal. "Okay. We have placed our weapons on the floor. Let's talk this out—"

The barrel of a rifle snaked around the corner of the doorway, strafing the room with bullets. One caught the security guard in the shoulder, and he bellowed with pain. A Scarpoint soldier rounded the doorway, his eyes widening as he saw Rylan still standing. Marat was behind him, pistol in a double-handed grip.

Rylan fired the tranquiliser rifle, the dart catching the merc between the eyes. The drug's effect was near instantaneous. He dropped like a sack of dirt, eyes rolling back in his head. With no time to reload, Rylan closed the distance to Marat.

The Scarpoint officer squeezed his trigger, bullet ripping through Rylan's upper abdomen. Fired from such close distance, the round punched front to back, twitching her body like she'd been hit with a hammer. She pushed on with a cry of rage and smashed the stock of her rifle into Marat's face before he could get off a second shot. His cheek bone crunched on impact and she followed it up with a second blow to his solar plexus, taking the wind out of him.

Marat collapsed to his knees, mouth gasping for air. Rylan grabbed a handful of hair and flexed his neck backward, forcing him to meet her eye.

"This is for killing me earlier." Rylan rammed his face onto her knee and the merc hit the tiles, out cold. She staggered backward, a balled fist pressing into her abdominal wound.

"Boss, you okay?" asked Carter.

Rylan grimaced, sucking air between her teeth at the pain. "I'm fine." At least, she would be in five or ten minutes. No matter the countless times she'd been shot, it always hurt like a bitch.

Carter pulled some zip-tie cuffs from the soldier's pocket and restrained them both. Rylan leaned down, biting her lip against the pain, and ripped the dart from the soldier's forehead. She stared at his chest and saw the slightest rise. He was still breathing, but only just.

"He needs naloxone."

Carter grabbed a prefilled syringe from the cupboard. Removing the cap, he stabbed the needle through the soldier's pants into his thigh and depressed the plunger. Within a few moments, the man's breathing improved, and Carter left him in the recovery position to tend to the security guard's wound.

By the time Carter had wrapped a field dressing around the guard's shoulder, Rylan felt ready to move again. It still felt like a hot poker through her middle, but she was no longer bleeding, and knew the muscles and organs were starting to stitch together. She gingerly touched the wound under her shirt and winced. New tissue plugged the hole, but the skin was yet to grow across the surface.

"My boys are going to kill you for this." Marat spat a glob of blood on the floor and struggled to his knees. His left cheek had doubled in size, the eye half-closed with swelling.

"You can try," said Rylan. "But I don't like your chances." She grabbed the plastic tie between Marat's wrists and pulled him to his feet. "You're under arrest for the attempted murder of a federal agent. You do not have to say anything, but if you do, it may be used in evidence against you."

Both agents were now fully armed, having taken a rifle and pistol each from the Scarpoint soldiers. Rylan slung the dart gun over her shoulder by its strap, turned Marat to the doorway and pushed him forward with the muzzle of her rifle.

"We're going down to the truck, where you'll order your men to stand down." She leaned forward, lips close to his ear. "And if you fuck me over—I'll lodge a bullet in your skull. Got it?"

Marat stared defiantly ahead, saying nothing.

Rylan shoved him into the hall, knowing the evening was far from over. The chance of Marat's squad surrendering was close to zero. Faced with the prospect of decades behind bars, she'd bet good money they'd try to fight their way clear.

***

Rylan reached around the corner, found the switch and turned off the lights in the reception, plunging the room to darkness. Due to the windows on the far side of the room, from here on, they might be seen by Scarpoint soldiers outside. Holding Marat as a body shield, she moved into the main room and peered over his shoulder. Only half of the truck was visible through the glass, and aside from Anton and the keeper, there wasn't a single person in view. Rylan swore under her breath.

"How many in your squad?"

Marat shrugged. "I can't remember."

Rylan cracked her pistol against the side of her head. "Try again. How many are outside?"

Marat hocked a glob of bloodied spit on the ground, narrowly missing Rylan's shoe. "Four veteran soldiers." He bent his neck to the side, eliciting a dull crack from the vertebra. "And they answer to me alone."

"That's why you'll instruct them to stand down," said Rylan. She flinched back into the hallway as a round punched through the window, burying into the wall by her head.

"Did you see the muzzle flash?" asked Rylan.

"Back wheel of the truck," said Carter.

Rylan followed his line of sight and saw the edge of a boot disappear behind the rear wheel. Chances were, there'd be another taking cover at the front of the vehicle. She recalled the approach to the reception building, envisioning the firing positions likely taken by the enemy.

Rylan snatched the comm's radio from Marat's belt and brought it to her mouth. "This is Agent Sophia Rylan of the Australian Security Intelligence Organisation. Your operation is at an end. Your commanding officer is under arrest. Stand down and show yourselves."

Marat coughed a laugh. "They aren't going to listen to you, missy."

Carter flipped open a small case of the tranquiliser darts and extracted one. He rolled it between thumb and forefinger before raising the needle to the side of Marat's neck. The merc flinched away, eyes staring warily at the point.

"That's right," said Carter. "I'd be afraid as well. When I poke it through your jugular, carfentanil will stop your heart, and no-one's going to run for an antidote. Start co-operating before we lose patience."

"Raise the damn radio so I can speak," growled Marat. Rylan lifted the microphone before his mouth. "Stand down and form up before reception. That means all four of you."

The soldier who'd nearly shot Rylan stepped out from behind the end of the truck. Stony-faced, he carried his rifle in one hand to the prescribed point. Two other soldiers emerged from the shadows to stand in line.

"Is that all of them?" asked Rylan. She studied Marat's face, looking for signs he was lying. Marat stared straight ahead, expressionless.

"Aside from the soldier restrained upstairs and the one you killed, that's my entire squad."

Rylan clenched her jaw. If the prick was lying, at least they'd lowered the numbers of snipers in the dark. She poked the barrel of her pistol in the back of Marat's neck and shoved him forward. When no shots were fired at the move, she caught Carter's eye and indicated for him to follow. Rylan grabbed Marat by the shoulder, held a pistol to the side of his head and marched him to the exit.

Of the two glass panelled doors, one was propped open, a chill breeze gusting through the gap. Rylan paused, her heart skipping a beat. She'd been through similar situations in the past. Some had gone to plan, others had turned to shit.

She glanced over her shoulder at Carter. "Hang back. If I draw fire, mark its origin."

Rylan swallowed, steadied her hand and pushed Marat outside. A ramp descended in a switchback to the gravel road, lined by a waist high brick wall that served as a hand rail, and gave the benefit of cover to waist height from her front and left flank. Glancing to the right, she was blinded by a security light shining from the wall. If there was a sniper waiting, he would shoot from there.

Marat's soldiers stood on the road directly below. Although none of their weapons were trained upon her, each held a rifle with detached confidence.

"Drop your weapons and put your hands behind your head," ordered Rylan.

A guttural bark sounded, paws scrabbling in the dirt. Rylan glanced toward the animal keeper to see him straining against a thylacine's leash. The beast lunged towards the group of soldiers, dragging the keeper forward two paces. The man said something in a low voice and the beast settled somewhat but continued to watch with tail stiff and ears up. Anton stood behind the keeper with training remote in hand, looking as useless as an ashtray on a motorbike.

Rylan dragged her attention back to the soldiers. "Last chance. Drop your weapons or your boss gets a round through his knee."

"Not your call, miss," said one of the soldiers in a broad American accent. "We only stand down if the boss orders it."

Marat looked sideways, a satisfied smirk on his face.

The thylacine growled again. Reacting to the tension, it pulled on its leash, jaws snapping.

"Anton, use the damn control to calm it," snapped Rylan.

The manager's face was white as he stared at the remote, hands shaking. "Nick, which button do I press?"

The keeper strained against the thylacine, heels dragging forward in the dust. "The one labelled *'SIT'*," grunted Nick. "Top button on the left."

The soldiers watched the thylacine, weapons inching up under the beast's attention. Anton punched a button, and the control emitted a high-pitched shriek of a noise.

"The other left, you fool!" shouted the keeper. "That was the bloody attack order!"

The thylacine bristled at the noise and lunged hard, snapping the lead's attachment. The keeper dived forward, reaching for the collar. At the contact, the beast's attention switched to the keeper. Jaws clamped about his wrist, bones of the forearm breaking with an audible snap. Nick screamed as it dragged him to the ground, his cry of agony cut brutally short as the thylacine released the forearm and savaged his throat. Anton froze for a moment, a panicked fawn staring in the lights of a truck, and then he broke. Dropping the control, he abandoned his employee and sprinted for the nearest building.

Marat turned his swollen face to Rylan, crimson-stained teeth grinning.

"Don't you fucking do it," she growled.

Marat sneered and looked back to his soldiers. "ENGAGE!"

CHAPTER THIRTEEN

Rylan grunted as her right knee buckled inward. A neat entry hole punctured her pants on the outer side, the round tearing through the flesh of her quad muscles and out the far side. A split second later, the pain of the bullet struck home like a drover's brand.

Marat smashed his head back into her face, crunching her nasal bones like eggshell. Claret spurted from her nostrils, eyes watering as stars burst. Marat tore from her grip and charged down the ramp to his squad. With their officer free, the mercs opened fire.

Rylan let her leg crumple, hitting the concrete to take cover behind the brick wall. She bit her lip to stifle a scream, tasting copper as a tooth punctured mucosa. Stone chips flew, another round just missing her head.

"Shooter at three o'clock!" shouted Carter.

Rylan didn't need to be told. She'd seen the muzzle flash, a soldier on her unguarded flank. Unable to make out his shape against the security light's glare, she fired where she'd seen the muzzle flash and was rewarded by a gurgling scream.

A rough hand closed about her shoulder and Carter wrenched her back into the reception area.

"You get him?"

Rylan nodded, breathing in short grunts against the pain of her leg. Carter crawled behind the reception desk, and came back with a red first aid kit in hand. He opened the package and upended it on the floor, snatching a pressure bandage for snake bites from the pile. He quickly wound the bandage around her thigh by touch and tied it off, his attention still focused on the soldiers outside.

"Back to four of the bastards out there," he grunted. "How's the leg feel?"

Rylan pushed down on her thigh over the mid-shaft of the femur. Nothing crunched or moved, so she figured the bullet had missed the bone. "It's fine," she said through gritted teeth. It wasn't fine. In fact, it was *very* fucking far from fine. But knowing the pain would end helped her compartmentalise and shut it down.

Glass shattered in the conference room behind, bullets raking the area in a swathe of deadly hail. They were pinned down. The only options were attack or surrender, and Rylan didn't own a white flag.

Ignoring the pain in her thigh, she forced herself to kneel behind the wall, Carter joining her this time. Carter peeked over the wall and ducked again. Rounds punched into the brick work and zipped through the space where his head had been.

"Two mercs at either end of the truck," he said, voice tight with adrenaline. "Thylacine's eating the keeper. Didn't spot Marat or the other soldiers."

Shit. "Anton dropped the control earlier, is it still on the ground?"

Carter shrugged. "Didn't see it."

Rylan peered over the wall and spotted the control, lying where Anton had abandoned it on the road in panic. Unfortunately, Marat's squad had just made the same discovery. A soldier darted from cover at the back of the truck. Rylan fired at the gravel before the control, hoping to scare him off. It didn't work. The soldier skidded to a stop, snatched the plastic box off the ground and sprinted for cover again.

"Hold your fire!"

Rylan ground her teeth at the voice. It was Marat.

"Or the manager dies."

Rylan glanced over the wall and swore. Marat stood behind Anton with a gun to his head, using him as a shield. After everything Anton had done to destroy Naturtech and derail its research, she was inclined to let the man die. Rylan turned, taking the brief lull in fighting to search the surrounding area for their next move. They couldn't stay in their current location. They needed a better firing position, an opportunity to turn the game in their favour.

Marat extracted the recovered control from his jacket and pressed a button. A whistle sounded, and the feasting thylacine lifted its head from the keeper's gut. It stared for a moment at the Scarpoint officer, then trotted over with an expectant look upon its face. For a beast matted in arterial crimson, it had the expression of a tame German shepherd.

"Open crates one to three," shouted Marat.

One of his soldiers climbed onto the tray to access the control panel. He tapped a few buttons, and three locks sprang open with a metallic clang, allowing the gates to swing open a crack. Wet noses nudged through the gaps, followed quickly by muscled bodies that pushed the doors wide. The freed thylacines jumped down to the road and padded up to their sibling. They licked blood from its face and jowls, low yips sounding between the animals.

Marat pressed the original button again, and the new animals sat obediently before him. He looked at his squad. “Take the truck and remaining thylacines to the ship as planned. I’ll mop up here and follow. Move!”

A few seconds later, the truck’s engine roared to life, flood lights soaking the road in white light. Rear wheels spun and it jerked into motion.

“What’s the call, boss?” asked Carter. “We can’t just let them go.”

No shit.

Rylan glared at him for a moment, her mind racing for a plan. “We split up. You follow the truck and make sure those animals don’t leave the state. I’ll deal with Marat.”

“And leave each other without backup? I’m not going while you’re wounded.”

“I don’t have time for this crap,” growled Rylan. “I don’t need a babysitter, Carter. I’m your superior officer. Move your arse and tail that fucking truck.”

Carter grit his teeth but nodded. He did a quick check of ammunition and weapons then peered over the edge of the wall toward the security vehicle. “Were the keys left in the ignition of that Jeep before?”

Rylan thought back to the ride given to her earlier in the day, a time that seemed a decade before now. “I think so. Worth a shot, otherwise you’re stuck with our car,” she said, passing him the keys to the hire car.

Carter pocketed them. "Give me some cover, yeah?"

Rylan fired above the wall, her round spurting gravel next to Marat and Anton's feet. Marat flinched down, hiding behind the terrified manager. Carter took off, sprinting down the ramp's incline before vaulting the end. He scooped up the duffle bag from the edge of the road and sprinted for the Jeep.

A high-pitched beep sounded from Marat's controller, drawing Rylan's attention. She turned back in time to see one of the thylacines sent in pursuit. Tiny puffs of dust lifted from its paws as it sprinted after Carter, jaw hanging open in anticipation. The agent glanced behind him as he reached the Jeep, eyes opening wider on spotting the beast in pursuit. He grabbed the handle, and Rylan's heart stuttered with relief when it opened under his hand. Carter dived in as the thylacine caught up. He kicked out as the beast lunged into the driver's seat, boot catching the animal in the chest and throwing it backwards. Carter slammed the door shut before the animal could right itself and attack again. A second later, the Jeep's engine roared to life, and it took off down the road, around a bend and out of sight, the thylacine sprinting after.

Now it was down to her and Marat. Instead of the rifle, she picked up the dart gun. Sighting quickly over the low wall, she fired at the nearest animal. The thylacine yelped as a feathered dart lodged in its neck. It hit the deck, hind leg kicking at the site to try and dislodge the offending implement. Within seconds, the sedative took effect and it fell still.

Marat swore, cursing her in a language she didn't understand. He aimed a laser pointer upon her, and as Rylan quickly reloaded, the high-pitched attack order squealed from Marat's controller. The remaining two animals leapt into action, streaking toward her. Rylan switched aim to the leading beast and fired, hitting the animal centre chest. Knowing there wouldn't be time to reload again, she dropped the dart gun and reached for the rifle.

A cold barrel jutted into the back of her neck.

"Drop it!"

Rylan swore viciously but placed her rifle on the ground. One of Marat's soldiers had circled back through the building. He pulled her to standing, forcing her to take weight on the injured leg. Bleeding had ceased, but the muscle still hurt like a fresh wound. The thylacine jumped the wall and padded forward, lips pulled back with a snarl on its lips. Huge, the beast had to weigh at least eighty kilos.

"Boss, call it off, yeah?" The soldier backed a step away from the animal, dragging Rylan with him.

A soothing tone echoed from Marat's controller. The thylacine's ears perked up, and it trotted away. The other two animals lay still, their chests barely moving. The soldier pushed her forward, pistol in the small of her back. Rylan stumbled as pain lanced through her thigh. Refusing to show weakness, she minimised her limp and kept her face blank.

Marat kept the laser pointer fixed on Rylan's chest as she approached. The last thylacine's attention stayed upon her, tail straight and stiff, a low growl on its lips. Marat raised a hand to his face, fingers tracing his injuries. The left eye was swollen shut, nose deformed and trickling blood over his lips.

"You're looking *good*, Marat," said Rylan, voice thick with sarcasm. "Although your modelling days might be behind you."

"A broken nose is nothing." Marat grabbed the deformed nasal bones between his thumb and index finger and wrenched them straight. Rylan winced at the crunch. A jet of blood gushed from his nose, soaking into the top of his white business shirt.

"But the eye pisses me off; I think you broke the fucking socket. That's going to take surgery, you bitch."

Rylan laughed. "Seeing double, are you?"

A crack in the orbital floor could trap muscles of the eye, resulting in asymmetrical movement between the globes. Marat stepped forward and punched her in the guts.

"I'll take that as a yes," gasped Rylan, winded.

"Anton, how many thylacines are left?"

"Capable of taking commands?" said Anton hesitantly, his eyes fixed on the two inert beasts on the ground. "Ah, there's another three in the enclosure we'd yet to load."

"Good. There's time for one last training session before we leave." Marat glanced at his watch. "Move Miss Rylan to the enclosure, she's about to learn what happens to people who attack a Scarpoint officer."

***

Carter stamped on the accelerator, frustrated by the car's poor acceleration. Although the Jeep's exterior looked the part of a rugged workhorse, the engine had the heart of a foal and barely enough power to climb a steep incline. Frigid air whipped through the open sides, needling exposed skin mercilessly. He glanced at the rear vision mirror and cursed to see the thylacine in dogged pursuit, gaining on him with every stride.

The Jeep's headlights illuminated the gate ahead. It slowly rattled closed as the Scarpoint truck accelerated from the other side. Carter swore as realisation struck—even if he made it through the dwindling gap, he couldn't allow the thylacine to escape the property in his wake. Carter drew his pistol and turned in his seat. He swallowed, seeing the beast less than ten metres behind the vehicle. Carter squeezed the trigger twice. Dirt spat between the thylacine's paws, the second round cut the left ear to ribbons.

The thylacine jumped, landing in the back seat of the Jeep in an ungainly mess. The car lurched sideways, rear wheels sliding on the gravel as they rounded a last bend toward the gate. Carter recoiled from the slavering jaws of the beast and flicked his gaze forward. They were about to leave the road, heading straight for a tree. He dropped the pistol and lifted his foot from the accelerator, took the wheel in both hands and turned into the slide. The wheels gripped and the rear of the car righted itself, back end kicking violently. The thylacine righted itself, back claws slicing through the seat covers as it scrabbled for purchase. It lunged forward with jaws wide, slavering for the side of Carter's neck.

He hunkered away from it and the beast was left with a mouthful of the driver's seat instead, tearing fabric and yellow padding free.

BANG!

The right front tyre exploded, torn to shreds by a rock. The steering ripped from Carter's grip, front wheels turning hard lock to the right. The front suspension dipped, left corner of the fender dug into the dirt and the car flipped. Carter's body wrenched against his seatbelt as the windscreen exploded. Glass and dirt sprayed over him as the Jeep tumbled violently in a groan of crushed metal, rolling three times before coming to a stop on its roof. The roll bar protecting Carter's head was scratched and battered, but it had done its job, preventing him from being mashed like roadkill. He hung from his seatbelt, dazed and disoriented. Carter's head ached, his body hurting in a hundred places from banging against the interior of the car as it flipped. He eventually found the locking mechanism and released his belt, dropping with a pained grunt onto his shoulder. Carter crawled out of the wreck and got to his feet, eyes searching the surrounding bush for the thylacine.

A howl sounded to his right. He patted his waistband for the pistol, coming up empty as he turned toward it. But he had no need of the weapon, not anymore. The howl turned to a high-pitched whimper. The thylacine had been thrown clear of the wreckage, only to land onto the carcass of a dead tree. Impaled on a branch, it moved weakly, trying to extricate itself. Carter returned to the car, found the pistol he'd dropped and put the creature out of its misery, cursing Marat and Scarpoint.

If there was one benefit to the modern battlefield, it was the near absence of animals dying at the hand of man, confused and in pain. And now here they were again, creating an animal that shouldn't even exist, an animal bred only to kill, bleed and die at the direction of its master.

Carter spat a foul taste from his mouth and tapped his jeans pocket for keys to the hire car. He had to move quickly for any hope of catching the truck. Carter opened the glove box and found a security swipe to activate the gate, and ran for the car he and Rylan had arrived in.

Placing the car in gear, he stamped on the accelerator. Wheels spun a half turn before taking grip and lurching forward. Warmth trickled from his hairline and he wiped it away with the back of his hand, smearing blood across his forehead. Carter bit his lip, trying to decide which direction to take at the highway. The truck was headed for a dock, but which one?

Arriving at the T-intersection, Carter made a snap decision and headed in the direction of Hobart. With any luck, they would be heading for the main shipping terminal. But if he was wrong… Carter clamped down on his anxiety. He'd made a decision, and would have to pray it was correct.

CHAPTER FOURTEEN

The throbbing agony of Rylan's thigh had begun to settle. She flexed the muscle to test its strength, and was rewarded with a sharp pain. Having suffered similar wounds a hundred times before, Rylan was able to gauge the stage of healing easily. It would take her weight well enough, but would still hurt like hell if she needed to run. Under her bloodied pants, pink new skin would have sealed the wound, however, the muscle fibres of her quads had yet to fully knit.

Rylan sat upon a wooden dining chair. Tall-backed, wooden slats crossed behind her spine, while her arms lay upon raised armrests. Plastic zip-ties fastened each ankle to a chair leg, and her left wrist to the armrest. Her right hand had been left free, although a gun aimed at her head from above halted any attempt to free herself for the moment.

A rich organic smell of dirt and decaying leaves filled her nostrils. Instead of a dining room, her chair sat in the open. Eucalypt trees reached for the sky, interspersed by tussocks of native grass and fern. At a glance, the scene was that of any temperate Tasmanian rainforest, but a closer look noted the spacing of plants was too exact. Too well planned to be a product of nature. A clear roof arced high above, while the walls to either side were constructed of steel sheeting. She'd seen a similar building the previous day during her tour of the joeys' enclosure, however, something told her she wasn't about to be surrounded by infant thylacines. No, she was in the haunt of the adult pack.

Soft foot-falls approached from behind, barely making a noise over the wet ground. Rylan flared her nostrils, taking a deep breath. A slightly rancid smell overlay the organic aromas now, notes of rotting meat and sweaty musk.

The smell of a carnivore.

A low soothing tone came from above and four adult thylacines padded into view. With Rylan seated, they stood tall as her chin, their shoulders and torsos broad, muscular and striped. The beasts observed her, padding in slow circles as if deciding which part to eat first. One came forward slowly and sniffed up her thigh towards her groin.

"Go on, get out of it," she growled.

The beast flinched at her voice, lips snarling to expose finger-length incisors. It snapped the air in front of her face in defiance, then slunk back to its pack mates.

A low chuckle sounded from above. Marat stood on a raised steel walkway at the edge of the enclosure, four metres above the ground and safely out of reach. Anton hovered to the side of the Scarpoint officer, his face the colour of curdled milk.

"I do believe they like you, Miss Rylan," said Marat. "Give it a few more minutes and I'll ensure you become properly acquainted."

"Cut the crap and get me out of here, Marat," said Rylan.

She might as well have been talking to a brick wall for all the attention he paid.

"Anton, how big is this enclosure?" asked Marat.

The manager came to the railing, looking like he was about to vomit. “Ah… This building opens onto three acres of fenced bushland. The animals can roam during the day, but we lock them inside at night.”

Rylan stared ahead. Twin doors were pinned back already, spilling light onto a few paces of bush. Beyond that, the rest was lost in darkness.

“These magnificent animals have taken human prey,” said Marat, staring down at Rylan. “Now it’s time to introduce the challenge of a soldier, and what better than a warrior such as yourself, with over two hundred years’ experience.” Marat smiled, his swollen face creating a grotesque parody. “Now, most of their future targets will be armed in some way; as such, I’ll allow you a knife.”

Rylan coughed a laugh. Might as well give her a toothpick for the good it would do against one of these beasts. “Give me a rifle or at least a bloody handgun.”

Marat smiled condescendingly. “And hand you a weapon that could be used upon me? I’m not a complete fool.” He turned and pointed at one of the various CCTV cameras attached to the walls. “Anton’s informed me that cameras such as these are mounted throughout the enclosure, so wherever you make a final stand, we’ll be watching with great interest.”

Marat pulled a knife from a sheath at his belt and threw it with a practiced flick of his wrist. It cartwheeled through the air, landing point first in the soil by her right foot, close enough to reach with her free hand. With one eye on the beasts, Rylan retrieved the weapon. Taking her opportunity, she sliced the ties at her ankles and wrist before looking up at the mercenary. For a brief moment, she contemplated throwing the knife before discarding the idea. Contrary to Hollywood's lies, throwing a knife was nearly always a bad idea. The chance of it hitting point first were minimal, and that was even if she managed to hit the bastard. No, she'd have to find a way to survive and take him out in a different way. Rylan cursed herself, wishing she'd killed him earlier. Three fucking times she'd been shot in one damn night! Marat was going to pay with his life. Rylan stood slowly, testing her injured thigh with gritted teeth. It would do.

"You will have a forty-five second head start before I send the dogs in pursuit," said Marat, looking at his wrist watch. "Starting—now!"

Rylan sprinted for the door, adrenaline surging, breath harsh in her ears as she ran into the dark. After the light of the indoor enclosure, she could barely see a thing. Plants whipped past her legs, tugging at her jacket and feet. Seeing a low branch at the last second, she dodged sideways but it caught her in the shoulder, spinning her around to hit the ground in a sprawl of limbs. Rylan got to her feet, saw that there was a shorter straight branch next to the one with which she'd collided. She planted a foot against the trunk and wrenched upwards, snapping off a one metre length. The splintered end was a pointed spike, as close to a spear as she would likely find. Rylan's head flicked toward the sound of yipping barks.

Marat had released his war dogs.

Breath tight in her chest, Rylan glanced at the moon to orientate herself, then took off at a sprint, branches whipping past her face as she angled toward the enclosure's southern border. Her eyes had finally adjusted to the dark, rendering the bushland in greyscale under the moon. She dodged around a fallen log and skidded to a stop. A three-metre-tall cyclone fence blocked her path, topped by ringed coils of razor wire. There was no way to climb over, but if she could scale an overhanging tree, she just might drop to the other side.

Rylan scanned the fence in either direction and spotted a tall gumtree with a branch reaching to the far side of the barrier. It would be a nasty drop to freedom, but a shattered ankle was preferable to being eaten alive. Before she could act, movement in the undergrowth forced her attention. She glanced over her shoulder and spotted the lead thylacine closing rapidly.

Fuck.

There wasn't time to climb out of reach. Rylan stepped away from the trunk, keeping the tree to her back. Three thylacines sprinted through the bush toward her, their stripes blending with the shadows. Jaws gaped, huge canines white in the gloom. The barking of early had quietened as they closed for the kill, attention focused with hungry intensity. The beasts formed an arrow shape, the largest one leading on point. Rylan steadied herself, makeshift spear tight in her fist.

With less than five metres separating them, the first beast leapt, lips curled back in a silent snarl.

CHAPTER FIFTEEN

Carter pushed the hire car to its limits, tyres barely maintaining contact with the tarmac as he rounded a bend at speed.

Come on, where the fuck are you?

He swore at a car travelling well under the speed limit. A beige Toyota Camry blocked his path, the favoured model of so many elderly Australians across the county. He flashed his headlights for it to pull aside and give him room, but it continued on its way, either oblivious to his rapid approach, or stubbornly retaining its right to the road.

Carter stared past the car, seeing if it was possible to overtake. A blind bend approached, hiding the knowledge of oncoming traffic. He decided to gamble and pulled out. As he came even with the Camry, headlights peeped around the corner ahead. The cabin of a semi-trailer burst into view, its massive bulk filling the entire lane. Carter swallowed and stamped the accelerator to the floor. He was committed now. Luckily, the Camry driver beside him had seen the danger and hit his brakes. Carter swerved back into his lane with inches to spare, the truck passing with airhorn blaring.

Carter ignored the fact he'd nearly become a crumpled heap of meat and metal, and powered on, emerging from a long bend to see another truck ahead. Steel enclosures sat upon its tray, carrying the hybrid thylacines. Carter smacked his steering wheel with the palm of his hand, letting out a yell of excitement and relief that he'd caught up to them.

He lightened his foot on the accelerator, hanging well back from the truck as they entered the fringes of a small town called Dodges Ferry. Instead of continuing to Hobart and the city's main commercial port, the Scarpoint truck turned off the main road for Tiger Point Bay, eventually stopping at a smaller boat ramp and pier.

A mid-sized fishing trawler was moored at the pier's end. A wheelhouse sprouted from the forward third of the boat, while the rear deck had been cleared of fishing equipment, leaving a flat open area. The truck did a U-turn and backed down the ramp, rear wheels submerging beneath the water until its bumper nearly touched the trawler's stern.

Carter parked in the far end of the adjacent parking lot and switched off his lights, thanking his lucky stars he'd caught up with the mercs before they'd left the highway. He'd thought they were headed for Hobart's main port on the Derwent River, where the animals could have been loaded on a container ship destined for Europe. But such a port came with twenty-four hour surveillance, and in hindsight, an isolated location such as this made sense. It also meant they were probably transferring the animals to the mainland for a different route to the northern hemisphere, maybe via plane.

Three Scarpoint soldiers piled out of the cabin and climbed up to the cages. A worker on the trawler deployed a crane and sling, consisting of two lengths of thick chain tipped by self-locking hooks. One soldier clipped the hooks in place, then stepped back as the cages were lifted as a group.

They swung in a semi-circle to the trawler, where they were gently lowered and fastened to the deck.

Carter itched to attack. If the boat left port it would be all over, but experience told him to wait for a better opportunity. Two of the soldiers held defensive positions on the dock, surveying the near ground above their rifle sights. If he made a move now, his only option would be to open fire, guaranteeing a blood bath.

Might not have a damn choice soon.

Evidently satisfied no one was following, the soldiers left their post, boarded the trawler and disappeared below deck. The remaining soldier drove the truck back up the ramp towards the carpark and main road. Carter reached into the back seat and grabbed the duffle bag housing the grief-sucker, along with the rifle he'd stolen from the merc in the control room. Quickly, he slipped from the car and crouched behind the boot. The Scarpoint truck accelerated up the drive from the ramp. A large tree loomed to the left, ancient and broad across the base of its trunk. Carter sighted upon the front left tyre and squeezed the trigger. The tyre exploded with a bang and the wheel housing dropped onto the steel rim, causing the truck to skid to the left, straight into the tree.

Carter scooped up the duffle bag and sprinted for the dock. His shot would have been heard, leaving him only seconds to board. Carter paused at the truck to check on the driver and found him unconscious with a bloodied forehead, the windscreen cracked from the impact of his skull.

Carter grinned inwardly at his luck. *Should have worn your seatbelt, mate.*

The trawler's diesel engine had started, bubbles and turbulence turning the water behind its stern as the propeller burst to life. A worker stood at the bow, removing the last rope anchoring the boat to the pier. At the sound of the truck crash, he glanced over his shoulder, eyes widening at the sight of Carter sprinting toward the pier. He dragged the loop of rope off the bollard, dropped it on deck and ran to raise the alarm.

Carter finally hit the pier, timber slats thundering under foot. The boat engine revved, and the vessel inched away from the dock, the separating expanse widening within every second. He'd have to bloody jump. A merc threw open the door of the wheelhouse, saw Carter and raised his rifle.

"Halt, or I will fire!" he shouted.

Carter put on one last burst of speed, pumping his legs with everything he had. Bullets chewed into the slats by his feet, splintering the wood as he leapt. Salt air rushed past his ears and then he hit. His back heel clipped the gunwale, tipping him into an ungainly roll. Carter hit hard, stars sparking as his head clunked off the deck.

The duffle bag thrashed beside him, grief-sucker within furious at its treatment. The thylacines barked, lunging at the front of their enclosures with saliva frothing between their teeth. The pier was now twenty-odd metres behind him to starboard, the trawler moving into deeper water. Carter gained his feet with difficulty, injured ligaments in his right ankle threatening to give way.

The Scarpoint soldier had left the cover of the wheelhouse and thundered across the deck with rifle at his shoulder.

"Don't fucking move!"

Carter had lost his own weapon in the jump and saw it two paces away. He lunged toward it. A round whined past his left ear like a hornet, sparking off the metal decking behind.

Fuck.

He froze and held his arms out to the side, eyeing the approaching soldier warily from his knees. Carter needed to stall the guy, convince him to return to port.

"We need to talk. Your boss is breaking international laws—"

The soldier ignored him and kicked Carter onto his back. He grunted, gut muscles spasming at the impact point. The merc leaned over him, drew his rifle back and thumped the butt into his forehead.

Everything went black.

CHAPTER SIXTEEN

The thylacine leapt with jaws spread impossibly wide, a line of drool trailing from the side of its mouth. Rylan planted the base of the branch in the dirt, screamed an unintelligible war cry and braced for impact. The spike punched into the beast's chest, force of impact knocking Rylan off her feet and driving the wood deep. The branch snapped, leaving a hand-span protruding as the beast twitched in death on the ground.

Rylan rolled to her feet, focus already on the second incoming tiger. A fallen branch with a swathe of green leaves lay at her feet. She snatched it up, holding it before her body like a bull-fighter's cape. In her other hand was Marat's gift, the Ka-Bar knife. Unbeknownst to the merc, he'd gifted Rylan a weapon she'd used before. As a British Commando in the Second World War, she'd swapped her Fairbairn-Sykes knife for a US Marine's Ka-Bar, and it had stayed at her side for the remainder of the war. The knife in her hand was a near perfect copy to the one she'd carried. A single-edged, seven-inch blade protruded from a segmented leather stacked washer handle. Her fingers tightened around the ribbed grip, familiar as the touch of an old lover, and readied for a stabbing thrust.

Unlike the first thylacine, this animal ran straight at her, eyes fixed centre of mass. Rylan twitched the mass of leaves in front of her body, keeping the beast focused upon the movement as it charged. At the last second, keeping the branch in place, she stepped out from behind it to the side. The beast crashed through the thin span of leaves, glancing off her thigh with jaws wide. As it passed, Rylan pivoted on her heel and stabbed the Ka-Bar between its ribs. The momentum of the animal nearly tore the knife from her grip.

A ragged growl from the third creature reverberated through her chest. With no time to recover, the remaining thylacine crashed into Rylan's back, knocking her flat on her face. It was on Rylan in an instant. Front paws stood on her spine, its body weight holding her down as it lunged and bit at the side of her chest, jaw clenching like a bear-trap. The thylacine worried at its grip. Teeth sliced through her coat and punctured the skin below her breast, the underlying ribs snapping like balsa wood. Rylan screamed and stabbed blindly behind her with the knife. She felt the blade enter flesh, twisted the grip and stabbed again.

The thylacine let go, howling with pain. Rylan pushed herself up and scooted back until she felt the tree at her spine. Her breath came hard, every inhalation a stab of pain in her chest. Air sucked into the wound about the flail-rib segment, her chest tightening as a pneumothorax developed. Soon air would fill the space between lung and chest wall, causing her lung to collapse. If it progressed, it would compress her heart, stop it from pumping, and she'd become a thylacine banquet.

She needed to move.

Rylan tried to ignore the pain and scanned the area. The first thylacine was dead. Sightless eyes stared as blood leaked about the stake in its chest. The other two were badly injured, but alive. Standing a few metres back, the first eyed her warily. It swayed on its feet, blood dripping from nose and mouth. The second limped, blood matting the fur of its thigh.

"I'm the first prey to put up a fight, eh?" Rylan took no pleasure in their injuries and would have preferred to euthanise them with a dart, but nor did she plan on dying again.

She leaned forward and got to her knees, teeth clenched against the pain. A low moan escaped her lips as she climbed to her feet, a hand on the tree to keep herself steady.

Movement flickered in the shadows to the right and a fourth thylacine padded into the clearing. Instead of attacking, it growled at her as if in warning to stay away, and trotted up to its surviving pack mates to sniff their wounds.

Rylan bared her teeth in frustration, knowing she was in no state to fight. Any movement of her right arm shifted the broken ribs, re-tearing flesh to delay healing. From past fractures, she knew it required at least thirty minutes for a fracture to resolve, time that she didn't have.

Rylan held up the Ka-Bar in her left fist. "See this? My fang's bigger than yours, buddy, and I have a nasty bite. Just ask your brothers."

The beast growled, hackles raised over its shoulders. It took two steps closer.

"You look nervous," said Rylan, her voice low and menacing. "Never met another predator? Well, welcome to the human race. We kill. Fucking. Everything!" Rylan stamped forward, throwing her left arm wide to look bigger and roared at the beast, vocal cords straining. The bluff worked. The thylacine retreated, tail drooping in confused hesitation.

Rylan took the chance and began walking for the covered enclosure and Marat. Breathing was becoming difficult, each inhalation shallower than the last. She needed a cannula or even the empty tube of a pen, anything to puncture her chest and release the air building up inside. Every step caused the ribs to move, tearing healing flesh anew. If only she could lie down and let her body heal!

A shadowy movement registered in her peripheral vision.

"Keep your distance, buddy," she muttered, swiping her knife at them. Rylan immediately regretted the action, bones crunching in her chest. The surviving thylacines followed a few paces behind, spread in a loose arc.

Rylan splinted her ribs with an arm and coughed. Copper flooded her mouth and she spat a mouthful of crimson into the dark.

Pain is just fucking pain. Get on with it.

She wiped her lips with the back of her hand and marched for the compound.

CHAPTER SEVENTEEN

Carter's eyes opened, a shock of freezing saltwater waking him up. He spat brine and tried to blink the water from his eyes as he struggled to sit. A migraine gnawed at Carter's temple like a rat, blood leaking from a ragged scalp laceration courtesy of the rifle butt. Two mercs stood above him on the deck, one with an empty water pail in hand. Another soldier hung back, standing outside the wheelhouse.

"I hope you kissed your children goodbye," said the soldier with the bucket. "Because they're about to lose a father." The mercenary didn't look concerned at the prospect of murdering Carter; for such a man, the taking of life had acquired the mundanity of filing taxes—an annoyance, but something that couldn't be avoided.

Carter ignored him, instead taking a second to catalogue his injuries and work out what body parts he could trust. Carter's left eye was nearly closed, eyelid purple and swollen leaving a mere slit for vision. He wiggled toes and flexed the muscles of arms and legs. A sharp pain radiated from his lower back in an electric shock down his thigh. Carter grimaced annoyance. On top of everything else going to shit, his sciatica was back.

One of the soldiers patted him down for weapons. He extracted a knife from Carter's belt and placed it by the pistol and rifle they'd already confiscated. Carter glanced to the side, saw a thylacine snuffling with great interest at the duffle bag against its mesh cage. Following his line of gaze, the soldier retrieved the bag and dumped it on the deck.

"What's in this?"

"A violent little friend of mine." Carter frowned as a sour bubble of nausea rose in his throat, head aching like he'd downed a bottle of tequila. "Go ahead and open it, you boys would get along great."

The merc touched a hand to the knife at his waist, eyes hardening. "I could turn that laceration into a proper scalping." He glanced over his shoulder at his comrade. "What do you reckon, Jannie? It's been a while since we took a souvenir."

Carter shrugged. "Fine. It's ammo; take a look for yourself."

The soldier squatted and unzipped the duffle bag, staring inside for a moment before looking up with a puzzled expression. "It's empty? Could have sworn it had something in it a second ago."

Carter pulled his legs underneath himself as both soldiers looked into the bag again. There was a shimmer of movement, like clear water in a moving stream, and suddenly the soldier staggered back with blood spurting from his neck. Coated in scarlet, the grief sucker's features came into vivid relief as it savaged the man's throat.

Horrified, the second merc recoiled. Carter lurched to his feet and grabbed the grief-sucker by its slimy tail. Ripping it free, he swung it into the second soldier. The beast happily complied, wide mouth latching onto the man's face with serrated teeth as his colleague bled out.

Carter crouched, snatched his handgun off the ground and fired a round centre of mass into the merc with the beast on his face. He screamed and staggered back blindly, tripping over the dead man. The soldier fell, his skull mashing into the control panel for the thylacine crates. Lights above each of the crate doors flashed green, electronic latches unlocking with a dull clang.

Ah, fuck.

Carter's gut dropped as the first thylacine nosed open its gate and padded through the gap.

CHAPTER EIGHTEEN

Rylan staggered into the light. After the darkness outside, the fluorescent bulbs high above made her wince. She was struggling to draw air, each breath an effort. Light-headed, her vision turned grey at the edges. Marat and Anton stood barely ten paces away, waiting for her. The Scarpoint officer held the thylacine control with the confidence of a lion-tamer as his war dogs trailed her into the building. They had grown in confidence as her strength faded, closing on her heels. There were now but two, the beast with the chest wound having collapsed part way back.

The uninjured animal finally made its move, lunging forward to snap at her lower leg. Canines tore a strip of material from her pants along with a wad of bloody flesh. Rylan would have screamed, but she could barely draw breath. She swung an uncoordinated slash with the Ka-Bar, scoring a runnel across the thylacine's snout. It yelped and backed away to circle in from the other side. Blood dripped from its nose, bright under the lights.

"Miss Rylan, you do not disappoint," said Marat. Lacking any sarcasm, Rylan noted a grudging respect in the man's tone. "We need to introduce weapons to their training. I would be loath to accept such casualties in the future."

Rylan gasped for air and got nothing. Her chest was tight as a drum, unable to move air in or out. Strength faded from Rylan's legs. One moment she was standing, the next she was on her knees, torso swaying. She focused on Marat's face, refusing to give in to unconsciousness.

"Pneumothorax," she gasped, every word a torture. "Need cannula to… release the air."

Anton fidgeted at Marat's side. "Maybe we should help? If ASIO draws a line between her death and Scarpoint, they'll throw every resource at their disposal to bring you down."

"Careful, Anton," said Marat, his eyes dead. "That almost sounded like a threat."

Anton backed away, hands up in capitulation.

Marat finally laughed and looked down at Rylan. "Why would I fear ASIO? And besides, Miss Rylan will not be found. No one will be left to tell the story."

Rylan glanced at Anton, saw his eyes widen. *That's right buddy, you're a loose thread. Once Marat has his animals, you're no longer needed.*

Rylan tried to speak, but couldn't make a sound. Her diaphragm and intercostal muscles spasmed, trying in vain to draw air. She fell forward, ribs crunching agonisingly again as they hit the ground.

Padding footfalls came from the right until claws entered her peripheral vision. Hot fetid breath gusted over her bare neck, blood dripping softly to the grass by her face. The beast was above her, but she had no strength to move. Colour sapped from the world, and her vision died like a failing bulb in the dark.

***

Carter stood at the midpoint of the crates, two cages to either side of him. A large female rammed her door open, the steel frame crashing against the structure with a mighty clang. Carter fired two quick shots, one to the chest, the second into the beast's skull. It dropped like a sack of potatoes, dead before it hit the deck. Carter spun for the creature behind him, squeezing the trigger again.

It failed to fire.

There was no time to troubleshoot the cause, not with a huge thylacine lunging for his face. Instead of pulling the trigger, Carter smashed the gun into the creature's mouth, knocking a giant canine free. Unfazed, the beast snapped at the gun, teeth screeching against the metal barrel as it ripped the weapon from his grip.

Carter turned and ran, desperate for distance between himself and the thylacine. He glanced upward and made a snap decision to gain some height. Using an open door, he hauled himself up, scrabbling on top of the block of crates. The chasing thylacine snapped at his feet, missing his toes by a hair's breadth. It stood on hindlegs, front claws scratching for purchase.

Carter backed away, and spotted the remaining two thylacines on the far side of the block of cages. One caught sight of him and stood on its hindlegs as well, paws sliding off the edge without success. The other loped towards the wheelhouse searching for easier prey. On top of the crates, Carter felt naked and exposed. It was only a matter of time before one of the thylacines decided to jump on top of the crates, a height they should be able to easily clear. There was still another Scarpoint soldier on board, and standing up here doing nothing wasn't going to end the fight. Carter squatted, lifted his pants leg and extracted a knife from a sheath about his right ankle that the merc's brief pat-down had missed.

A screech of rusty metal sounded from the wheelhouse. Carter glanced up, and saw a hatch swing up and open on its roof. The end of a ladder appeared through the gap, soon followed by the head and shoulders of the last Scarpoint soldier. The merc drew a rifle up through the gap, his line of fire completely unobstructed. Carter threw himself to the side, rounds tearing through the air like hornets behind him. He slid off the crates and dropped to the deck.

And back to the damn thylacines.

Crates protecting his back from the soldier, Carter landed on the balls of his feet with knife in hand, ready as the first beast came for him. From the back of the trawler, it sprinted along the metal deck and jumped the last two metres, jaw gaping. Carter dropped to a squat and punched the blade up as the beast soared over his head. The point entered just below the ribcage, momentum unzipping the length of its abdomen against the knife's razor edge. It hit the deck howling and fell overboard in a tangle of limbs and bowel.

Carter knew he wouldn't get so lucky a second time. He needed some sort of shield, something with which to parry an attack. Carter shrugged off his jacket and wrapped it around his left forearm. The sounds of the dying thylacine had drawn the attention of its pack mate. This one approached more warily, lips pulled back in a snarl before surging the last few paces. Carter protected his face by shoving his left forearm into his mouth and stabbed around the side, blade deflecting off its scapula. The thylacine clamped down with the bite strength of an African lion. The padding did little to protect his arm, powerful jaws snapping radius and ulna like twigs.

Carter screamed, eyes wide, tendons standing proud on his neck. He stabbed wildly at the beast's neck, desperation lending strength to his blows. The creature's teeth finally sliced through the jacket material, tearing into the muscles of his forearm. Carter stabbed again, this time rewarded by an arterial spray as he severed a carotid artery. He kept stabbing until the thylacine released its hold. It staggered back and collapsed, blood pouring from a myriad of wounds. Carter cradled his mangled arm to his chest, biting his lip to keep himself from screaming.

For a moment there was nothing but the sound of waves, Carter's ragged breathing and the breeze moaning about wire stays. They had left the small towns of Dodges Ferry and Carlton behind. Dark bush lined the edge of the bay as the trawler headed for deep water. Footsteps upon the metal drew Carter's attention. He looked up and met the last soldier's eyes.

Carter's heart didn't beat any faster this time around. His adrenaline was spent, a sense of fatalism settling in his chest. He sighed and stood up straight, feeling nothing but exhaustion. The merc was pale faced and on edge, eyes wide. He paced forward slowly with rifle raised, the end of the barrel wavering slightly.

"Drop the knife," ordered the soldier in halting English. "Put your hands behind your head."

Carter obeyed. Letting the knife fall to the deck, he was careful to note where it came to rest. The merc approached again. A slight movement to the right of the soldier caught Carter's eye, the barest shimmer of distorted air. To avoid a pool of blood, the soldier stepped closer to the crate

A mistake he would regret.

Air aside the crate wall shimmered and suddenly blood was spurting from the side of the soldier's head, his ear ripped clean off. He yelled in surprise and fear, and reflexively squeezed the trigger of his rifle. At close quarters the noise was deafening. Bullets ricocheted off metal, buzzing past Carter until the merc dropped his weapon to rip the invisible animal off his face with both hands.

For a split second Carter did nothing, not daring to believe all the rounds had somehow missed his body. Finally, he lurched into action. Scooping his knife from the deck he closed ground to the soldier and plunged his blade into the man's heart. The soldier collapsed to the deck, joints unhinging as one. A bloody outline of the grief-sucker's mouth and teeth hovered over the soldier's head until a rippling flood of mucous washed the blood away. Near invisible again, it scuttled away and hid in a corner.

Carter took a knee, eyes closed against the pain of his mangled left arm. A yipping bark sounded from the back of the trawler, scrabbling claws on metal decking once again. Carter grimaced.

Come on, one more fight. You can do this.

He lunged for the merc's side arm but struggled to unclip the pistol from its holster. When he finally extracted the weapon, the beast was nearly on him. Carter rolled to his back and shot.

And missed.

The thylacine took another two strides and leapt, but not at Carter. It cleared the gunwale and landed in the bay with a splash, disappearing beneath a swell before popping up again five metres away. Carter gained his feet with a groan and leaned on the rail. He lifted the pistol and sighted on the animal. Already, it had gained some distance from the trawler, was over twenty metres away and angling for the distant shoreline. Carter began to press the trigger… then stopped.

He'd had enough of killing animals for one day.

"Please don't shoot."

Carter turned his head wearily, and saw two trawler crew standing at the door of the wheelhouse. "Are you the captain?"

The man nodded. "I didn't want a part of this, but Scarpoint blackmail—"

"Just turn the ship around." He wasn't in the mood to hear the captain's excuses. Until he knew Marat was behind bars or dead, the night was far from over. "Get us back to shore. Now!"

CHAPTER NINETEEN

Rylan gasped, taking a deep breath of fresh, cold air. It stung like razor blades through her expanding lungs, ribs still aching like a bitch in the right side of her chest. Rylan took another breath and realised the broken section of ribs no longer grated with the movement—they were starting to heal. A few minutes more and she might be able to trust them not to snap immediately. She glanced down, saw a cannula attached to a three-way-tap protruding from the second intercostal space, just below her collar bone on the right hand side. Air hissed out of it, draining the tension pneumothorax that had collapsed her lung and compressed her heart moments earlier. She was propped on the same wooden dining chair as earlier, although this time, was only fastened by her left hand. Evidently, Marat thought her injured enough to be of little threat. The pair of thylacines sat twenty paces distant, each still watching her intently.

"Glad to have you join us again," said Marat.

Marat walked into her line of sight and squatted, bringing them eye to eye, the thylacine control in his left hand. He pressed a button, activating the laser pointer so that a red dot appeared on her forehead again, reminding the thylacines of their target.

"What, no thanks for saving your life?" chuckled Marat. "Lucky for you, I have the training to deal with battlefield wounds. Nowadays this isn't always the case. In the Ukraine, some of our Russian jailhouse conscripts can barely fire their rifle, let alone manage a sucking chest wound."

Anton stood behind Marat's shoulder, staring intently as if to assure himself that she was actually alive.

"Besides, after the trouble you've caused," said Marat, "I wanted you conscious when my pets begin to feed." He paused, and when she gave him no reaction, Marat narrowed his lips with annoyance. "They'll only eat a foot, maybe an ankle as well. Enough that it will take some time to heal and prevent you from absconding."

Rylan looked at Anton. "Marat is going to kill you. Now that he has a breeding pair, he doesn't need Naturtech, let alone you."

Marat stood up. "Actually, I preferred when you weren't speaking."

"You'll be dead within the hour, Anton," said Rylan, continuing her play for time. Strength returned with every breath, the static position allowing her ribs and lung to finally heal. Despite this, she sagged in the chair and feigned agony. "Come on, you're a smart man, *think* about it. Why would he leave a trail of evidence that can be erased with a bullet? You messed with the wrong people, Anton, and now you're going to pay."

The manager's face dropped a shade paler, hands shaking. "Is that true, Marat?"

The Scarpoint officer rolled his eyes. "For fuck's sake, don't tell me you're listening to her. I haven't got time for this shit." He pointed to the raised walkway. "Go up to the landing so I can finish the show."

Rylan took a deep breath and held it for a moment. The ribs ached, but they were solid. She was ready to fight. Leaving her head lolling forward, she glanced up from under her brow. Anton scampered, leaving through a side door of steel mesh. Clanging footfalls beyond told of him climbing a steel staircase to the observation deck. Rylan looked at Marat. He had turned side on to her, examining the controller.

"Anton! How do I get them to bite a specific body part?"

Fuck this shit.

Rylan sprang to her feet, holding the chair by her one bound hand. She swung the chair in an arc into Marat's back. Seeing her move in his peripheral vision, he hunched his shoulders to brace for the blow. The chair splintered on impact, legs snapping off, the structure reduced to kindling. Freed, Rylan kicked Marat in the back of a knee, driving him to the ground and followed up with a knee to the head.

The merc maintained his grip on the control, falling onto his elbows to protect it. He punched a finger at a button, setting off the high-pitched attack instruction before flinging the control aside. The thylacines barked, springing into action.

Rylan put a knee in Marat's back, pinning him to the ground as she stole the handgun from his thigh holster, raised it and fired. The gun kicked and the first creature stumbled, the bullet creasing the top of its skull, leaving a bloody rent in the scalp. Marat twisted underneath, knocking her to the side. She landed on her shoulder with a grunt. Marat drew his Ka-Bar, buried the blade in her thigh and used it to pull himself to his knees.

Rylan screamed, brought the gun around and fired again, taking Marat point blank in the guts. He jerked with the round's impact, blood spattering as the bullet tore out through his left kidney.

One of the tigers latched onto her foot, jaws clamped about the leather boot. Another went for her hand, ripping the gun from her fingers before she could shoot again, teeth turning her digits to a bloody ruin. The thick leather of her boot kept the teeth from her flesh, but she felt bones snap under the pressure. Rylan kicked out with her other foot, stamping against its nose. Once. Twice. It let go for a moment and Rylan took her chance, diving to where Marat had thrown the control. She needed to redirect the thylacines' anger.

She grasped the control, came up rolling with it in hand and pressed the button to deploy the laser. Nothing. Three long cracks traversed the casing on top, while the back was stoved-in. *The fucking idiot.* Marat had destroyed the one means to control the thylacines when he had thrown the control aside.

Rylan turned, and saw Marat had climbed back to his feet. He hunched forward, a fist pushed into his wounded abdomen.

"Broken, is it?" Marat squatted with a pained expression to retrieve his gun. "I'll just have another made." He lifted the pistol and fired.

She staggered backward, leg buckling as she stood on her broken foot. Pain bloomed in Rylan's gut, joining the symphony of tortured body parts. Rylan regained her balance, a growl of anger and pain.

Marat lifted his fist, displaying his own bullet wound. "Only fair I returned the favour."

Movement in Rylan's peripheral vision took her attention, and she swung the control to meet the lunging thylacine. The casing cracked further, splintering as it collected the beast in the face. It backed away, circling in to attack from the other side.

Another bullet hit, this time in her left shoulder. The broken control dropped from nerveless fingers. Rylan groaned and fell to her knees.

"I was only going to take a foot," muttered Marat, his face ashen from blood loss. "Now I have a mind to let them feast."

"Sadist," spat Rylan. "You're a dead man, mark my fucking words." When her body was whole, she would make him pay. If she had to chase him to the battlefields of Ukraine, she would find and kill him.

Marat gave a humourless smile. "Not today."

He stepped back, making way for the two thylacines to approach. Rylan clenched her jaw, staring at the two animals. Both took their time, the smart bastards understanding she was incapacitated, defenceless. Finally, she closed her eyes and waited for the first bite.

A discordant whistle sounded from the walkway. Rylan opened her eyes and saw that the thylacines had sat on their haunches, eyes fixed upon Anton above. The manager held two whistles and a laser pointer.

"What the fuck are you doing?" growled Marat.

Rylan's heart lurched. She recognised the discordant note now, it was the same one Anton had demonstrated in the initial training of the joeys, a direction to change target. The manager raised the laser pointer in a shaking hand and depressed its button, casting a red line toward Marat. A crimson marker dot appeared on his forehead. The thylacines stood, tails stiff behind them, attention now fixed on the Scarpoint officer.

Marat slapped at his forehead as if he could erase the marker. "Get it off me, you fool. Aim it at Rylan!" There was a note of desperation, panic making his voice crack. "Now, or I'll see you dead as well!" He jerked his gun up at Anton.

Anton gave a small shrug. "You were going to kill me anyway." He raised the second whistle to his lips and blew. The high-pitched attack order tore at Rylan's ears. Marat fired, his round taking Anton in the shoulder as he dove aside. Marat turned the weapon on the thylacines as they attacked. Dirt spat between the first one's paws and then they were on him.

Rylan forced herself to stand, torn muscles and broken bones screaming for her to stay still. She bit her cheek and stumbled to the exit Anton had used earlier. By the time she swung the door closed, Marat's screams had stopped, replaced by the grotesque sound of feasting.

CHAPTER TWENTY

Naturtech's security gate stood open, an Australian federal police car parked alongside. Carter wound down his driver's window and held his ID badge for the approaching policeman. The constable was pale and on edge, a slight jitter to his hand as he took the ID and examined it for an inordinate amount of time. Looking all of twenty-one years old, he'd not long escaped the academy.

"Mate, you saw me last night," said Carter. "I've got shit to do and countless reports to write." After the past forty-eight hours he was exhausted and in no mood to deal with a greenhorn's nerves.

The officer bristled, but passed back the ID and waved him through. Carter put the car in drive and continued down the narrow dirt road until a police cordon forced him to stop. He parked, got out and ducked under a fluttering line of blue and white tape. The various buildings of the Naturtech facility were a stone's throw away. Agents, federal police officers and forensic technicians swarmed the site.

Yipping and muted whines emanated from a white van with 'Sorell Council Animal Management' printed in wide block letters along its side. Carter peered through a tinted window and saw roughly twenty joeys crammed in the back. A rusted metal grill separated a policeman in the driver's seat from the animals. He sat behind the steering wheel with a checklist balanced on his knee.

"Where are you taking them?" asked Carter. "I thought hybrid stock were to be euthanised."

"Nah, just the adults. These lucky buggers are taking a flight to Canberra."

"What're they going to do with them?"

The man shrugged. "No idea."

Carter worried the army may continue Scarpoint's program. He would rather the animals meet a gentle death at the end of a needle than subject them to such a life. Hopefully Rylan would be able to pull a few strings to ensure it didn't happen.

He gave the officer a nod and walked past the entrance to the adult enclosure, suppressing a shudder as he recalled what he'd found in there the previous morning. Despite pushing the trawler to maximum speed on the return trip, it had been nearly three o'clock in the morning by the time he'd made it back to Naturtech. Marat had been reduced to a pile of bones and offal. Anton had been a wailing mess, and Rylan barely conscious, soaked in blood. He had quickly euthanised the remaining adult thylacines with double doses of carfentanil. Soaked in gore and bellies distended, they'd looked something out of a horror movie.

Carter glanced at the setting sun, an icy breeze tugging at his unkempt hair. Despite the clear sky, the afternoon had been bitterly cold. He headed for the main building where Rylan had made an operation's hub. Carter steered clear of the entry ramp, leaving a forensic tech to pick bullet fragments from the concrete, and headed for a second entry point, finally finding Rylan in the conference room.

"Close the door behind," said Rylan without looking up. She sat at a table, notes in a jumble and a laptop open.

"How are you feeling, boss?"

At his voice, she finally looked up. Rylan appeared tired, but little different to normal.

"Alright, I guess. But the hand's taking its sweet arse time to resolve." She pulled a leather glove off and held up the fingers of her right hand. The index and middle finger looked raw and irritated, the skin red as a freshly cooked lobster.

"Damn sight better than yesterday at least," said Carter. To begin with, they'd been nothing but a mush of fractured bones, lacerated skin and tendon.

"And you? How's the arm?"

Carter shrugged. "I've had worse," he said. Technically that was true. The IED blast that had seen him medically discharged from the SAS had laid him out for months in hospital. But it didn't stop his new injury from hurting.

He glanced down at his left forearm, concealed within an above-elbow plaster back-slab; he hadn't been able to fit the damn thing in his jacket sleeve. The whole thing itched like a madman, and there was a throbbing ache at the fracture sites that beat in time with his heart. Luckily, the lacerations from the thylacine's teeth had been relatively shallow, prevented from cutting too deep by the jacket he'd wrapped around the forearm. A nurse practitioner at the Hobart Royal Hospital emergency department had washed out the wounds, given him antibiotics and cast the arm. He'd have formal surgery once he returned to Canberra the following morning. Carter glanced at his boss, wishing he had a touch of her healing ability.

"Scarpoint has denied all involvement," said Rylan.

"But we've got two of their men in custody and the DNA of others."

Rylan shrugged. "They claim Marat and his squad went rogue months ago."

"I call bullshit," said Carter.

Movement out the window caught Carter's eye. He looked up to see the animal management van drive away. "I heard the joeys are destined for Canberra. Please tell me they're not going to the ADF."

"Come on, Carter," said Rylan. "Have some faith; as if I'd let defence get their hands on them. No, I've donated the joeys to another agency seeking to resurrect the Tasmanian tiger. As much as Anton stuffed up here, Naturtech pulled off some ground breaking stuff, it would be criminal to ignore their findings. Introducing true thylacines back into the Tasmanian bush is now a real possibility."

Carter winced, thinking of the hybrid he'd last seen swimming for the shoreline. "Talking of releasing animals back into the wild... One of the adult females jumped ship. There's a chance it might have swum ashore."

"And you're telling me this *now*." Rylan fixed him with a glare before finally sighing. "If it's just the one animal, I suppose it doesn't matter. Without a breeding partner, it'll die and bring the hybrid line to an end."

Well. As long as it wasn't pregnant already.

Carter pushed the thought aside and wandered to a drinks cart in the corner of the room. Ignoring a pot of plunger coffee, he extracted a battered hip flask from his jacket and poured a dram into two mugs. Reduced to one hand, he took two trips back to the table with the mugs before sitting down opposite his boss.

"Are we going to address the elephant in the room?"

Rylan swished the whiskey about her mug for a moment before taking a sip. "This isn't bad," she said with an appreciative nod.

"It's a Lark single malt, but don't change the subject," said Carter. "What are we going to do about Friedman? If the bastard's got a contract on your head, it's only a matter of time until another squad comes for you."

"Well, they can try." Rylan took another sip before setting the mug down. "But I don't plan on giving them the chance."

Carter leaned forward slightly, waiting.

"I did some digging and found the location of his various private compounds. It just so happens, Friedman will be flying to a property in Puerto Rico to escape the winter. After we wrap up this case, I'll be taking six weeks of leave to pay him a visit."

"You'll want some back up," said Carter. "Infiltrating an armed compound takes more than one person, and I happen to have some excess leave that could be spent in the Caribbean."

Rylan said nothing for a moment. "You sure?"

"The bastard's had you shot several times, of course I'm fucking sure."

Carter gulped the rest of his mug, then pulled the flask from his jacket and poured another measure. He raised the cup and caught Rylan's eye.

"To Friedman's death."

The End

Check out other great

Cryptid Novels!

Edward J. McFadden III

THE CRYPTID CLUB

When cryptozoologist Ash Cohn receives a gold embossed printed invitation inviting him to join The Cryptid Club, he sees the resolution to all his problems.Famous cryptid scientist and biologist, Lester Treemont, one of the world's richest men, and the leader of the Cryptid Club, is dying. What he offers via his invitation is a chance to succeed him. To take over his wealth, laboratory, and discoveries. All Ash has to do is beat eight others like him in a series of tests both mental and physical involving Treemont's collection of cryptids. Seems simple enough, and Ash has nothing to lose.Nine strangers from across the globe, all with reasons for wanting to win. When they start dying one by one, the competition shifts to one of survival. Who among them will rise to the top and reign over The Cryptid Club?

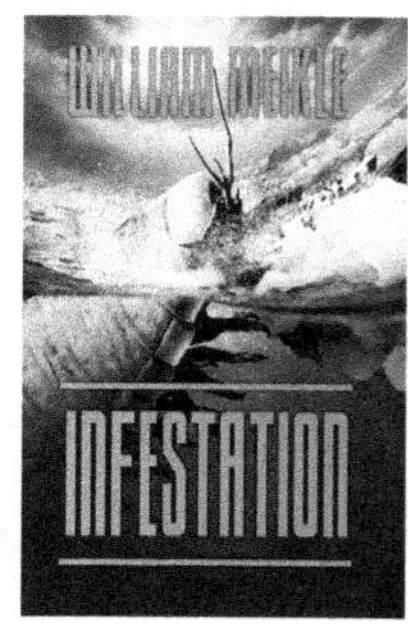

William Meikle

INFESTATION

It was supposed to be a simple mission. A suspected Russian spy boat is in trouble in Canadian waters. Investigate and report are the orders. But when Captain John Banks and his squad arrive, it is to find an empty vessel, and a scene of bloody mayhem. Soon they are in a fight for their lives, for there are things in the icy seas off Baffin Island, scuttling, hungry things with a taste for human flesh. They are swarming. And they are growing. "Scotland's best Horror writer" - Ginger Nuts of Horror "The premier storyteller of our time." - Famous Monsters of Filmland

www.ingramcontent.com/pod-product-compliance
Lightning Source LLC
LaVergne TN
LVHW020047110826
845155LV00029B/659

* 9 7 8 1 9 2 2 8 6 1 6 6 5 *